Beyond the Wide World's End

Meta Mayne Reid

Beaver Books

... To the wilderness I wander ...
I summoned am to tourney
Ten leagues beyond
The wide world's end—
Methinks it is no journey.

Tom o' Bedlam

With thanks to Grandmother Moody
whose work box gave me the idea
for this story

First published in 1972 by Lutterworth Press
Luke House, Farnham Road, Guildford
Surrey, England
This paperback edition published in 1976 by
The Hamlyn Publishing Group Limited
London · New York · Sydney · Toronto
Astronaut House, Feltham, Middlesex, England
Reprinted 1976

© Copyright Meta Mayne Reid 1972
ISBN 0 600 39362 3

Printed in England by Cox and Wyman Limited
London, Reading and Fakenham
Line drawings by Antony Maitland
Cover illustration by Neville Dear

Contents

Chapter One

ON THE WAY ALONE

Deep in the July night something awakened
Timothy. The mongrel terrier dog, Brandy,
lay quiet against him, the hay was soft below, the
peat reek hung in the air and coiled in the thatch
above his head. It seemed very far from the dream
of a boat bobbing on the river and a voice calling
from the jetty: "Timothy! Come for your supper,
boy." And at the sound of that call a dog would

dash down the steep fields to the river and dance
with impatience until his master came home for
supper beside the fire which Uncle Alexander
Erskine never allowed to go out, summer or winter.
Such a warm and welcoming place, that little farm
beside the wide silver river—he shut his eyes and
drifted back to it, passing in less than a second over
all the hundred or so of miles between County
Sligo and Foyleside.

But one word dragged him out of that well-loved
dream: his own name, spoken in the sharp, woman's
voice which in the past six months he had come to
hate. It spoke from the box bed which Timothy's
father shared with his new wife beside the living
room fire, below the open-ended loft.

"Timothy, is it? That brat! Now listen to me,
Will Maguire, I've put up with your cattle droving
for that's your living. I've shut my ears to the rough
side of your tongue when you're full and made do
with a pocketful of money one day and none the
next. I bargained for that. But Molly Erskine's
child—" She made a sound of disgust which
brought a rumbling protest from Timothy's father.

"I'll not hush. Let him go back where he belongs.
Either he goes or I'm off like a redshank." Her voice
sank to a low wheedling note. "It's me and my
wean you've to think of now, not a great lump of a
lad who's old enough to fend for himself. Let his
own kind take him now, and good luck to them, for
a hungrier, more long-leggity creature I never did
see."

There was the merest hint of a snore, but she was
not to be put off. "You'll not turn me with your

pretence. My mind's made up. Is it the lad or me?"

Timothy caught his breath, knowing what the answer must be. He heard rain spit down the chimney on to the glowing peats while he waited, and a curlew on its way to the estuary let fall its lonely liquid notes which made the world outside the known walls seem very wide and strange.

"Have it your own way," said his father at last. "Pity he's not four years older and could be off to fight Napoleon—that'd be an easy way out. But he's all Molly Erskine and nothing of me. He can go back to his own kin."

There was the sound of a smacking kiss. "That's my brave Will. Now we'll be thinking of the children to come and good-bye to Timothy."

Good-bye to Timothy. When the voices below ceased, he buried his face in Brandy's pelt and cried. Ever since his mother had died a year ago he had known this moment must come, yet could not believe it until the words were said. The tears carried him over the hump of the hill, he could accept what had been said, in what remained of the night could even begin to make plans and take stock. He was now almost twelve and tall for his age, born in the year of the 1798 Rising, in which his father had taken part.

The 1798 Rising in Ireland was of course a mere name to Timothy. He did not know that the Irish people had heard what great reforms the French Revolution had brought for the poor of France. Such news fired the Irish to rebel, hoping the English Government would grant equal rights of voting and choice of profession to men of all classes

and religions. The Rising failed for lack of organiza-
tion, but later British statesmen brought in laws to
join England and Ireland under one government,
and tried to help the poor and oppressed in both
countries. These laws were slowly bearing fruit,
but England, though now winning her long battle
with Napoleon Bonaparte, was still hard-pressed
and needed all the men and money she could
gather together to pursue the war, so Ireland's
troubles were forced to take second place for the
time being. The common people were desperately
poor and ill-educated, though the aristocracy and
the tradespeople flourished. But Timothy under-
stood very little of all this, except that his father had
been wounded in the Rising and been nursed by
Molly Erskine, who was to become his mother.
Together they had come back to Will's home near
Sligo. Here Timothy was born, son to cattle dealer
Will Maguire and Molly his wife, who was of
Foyleside farming stock. Timothy thought as much
about that farm as about the house he lived in,
for Molly had rued her bargain long ago and was
ever homesick.

The Maguire household had few intimates in
the neighbourhood, apart from their cousins and
next-door neighbours, the Kearneys. The youngest
cousin, Jane, was almost the same age as Timothy,
and his greatest friend. Being an orphan, she was in
even poorer case than he, for neither her grandmother nor her bachelor uncle cared for her except
as she was useful about the farm. Both Will and his
cousins boasted that they had once upon a time
seen better days and lived in bigger houses, so

because of their foolish pretensions many looked askance at the Kearneys and the Maguires.

Timothy grew up a lonely child, nourished on tales Molly told of that Foyleside farm, and the boat which was used for fishing on the broad river. There was an apple orchard too, and hazel bushes, and wild strawberries. It was perhaps not so unlike the Sligo cottage, except that there was love and kindness in it, but she made it seem like a child's wonderland, and Timothy knew which was the best pool for trout, the corner of the barn where the swallows nested, and even the kitchen stuff—down to the wrought-iron harnen stand, and the teapot which had a rosebud knob on its lid, the lustre jug and the A.B.C. sampler.

And now, he thought, I'll go back to it, and I'll take my few shillings and the shirt and breeches Mama made before she died last winter. I'll go back to where I belong. He felt he could hardly wait until daylight to make his escape. For of course he would go back of his own accord, rather than allow his father to tow him away like an unwanted puppy. But how he would miss Jane Kearney, and his own dog, Brandy. He tried to dismiss these aspects and to concentrate on his advantages.

How lucky that Mama had taught him to read and to figure, for on his journey he could read the milestones for himself; people were all too ready to think a lone boy on the road was an escaped prentice and hand him over to the nearest magistrate. There was the map too: Mama had made it to help his father in his cattle droving, and it showed all kinds of by-roads. Perhaps the distances were not always exact, but the general drift of it would at least help Timothy to steer his way across County Sligo and the small portions of Leitrim and Donegal until he came to County Fermanagh and had the big lake to guide him. That would be over half-way, and after that the roads were better and the way more direct. He would need food with him and a pack like a pedlar's. So, planning and thinking, he drifted late into sleep and had to be cuffed awake and dragged down the ladder when milking-time came. The poor cows were ill-tended that morning.

When at last he sat down to his dish of lumpy stirabout and buttermilk he watched his father warily, waiting to hear of the night's decision. He had forgotten that no dealer in his senses would miss the fair at Kilcracken. So it seemed that Timothy's affairs would be postponed until tomorrow. Indeed he was only given a hint of the midnight discussion when his stepmother declared she was going along with her husband: "For once the child's born, there'll be few jaunts for me. Timothy can stay behind today."

They set off, taking Brandy with them much against his will. Once his frustrated barks had died away Timothy was left alone to feed the fowl and the stock, to keep the fire up, to draw water from the well, make sure there was a stock of turf in the shed, and do the afternoon's milking if they should be delayed.

Once they were gone he could choose his tasks. The cattle and hens could forage for themselves. Turf and water could be brought in by anyone, but pigs in the sty could not roam after their own food, so he tipped swill into their trough, and saw that the turkeys in the fox-proof enclosure had water to drink before he started on his own business. He would have liked to talk to Jane Kearney but when he turned towards the Kearneys' farm he saw her grandmother busied about the door, and decided it was safer to keep away. But how strange life would be without Jane and Brandy. He took a deep breath and turned back into the house where there was no one to question as he went about his preparations. Clothes were no problem, for he had only one spare shirt and pair of breeches, and had outgrown his last brogues. Anyway the soles of his feet were tough as leather. He took the blue neckcloth which Mama had made for him out of the tail-end of her last weaving, also the striped blanket which he shared with Brandy; it would turn the rain and keep out the worst of the wind. He could wear it as a plaid, folded tightly and wound across from left side to right shoulder.

As for food, he must carry what he could and work—or even beg—for the rest. He helped himself to a heap of oatcakes which he plastered liberally with butter and wrapped in a piece of linen torn from a clean shift which had belonged to Mama (so did not count as stealing). He looked greedily at the hams hung among the rafters, cut little snippets from each and boiled them alongside a dozen eggs. The salt cod was no temptation, but he filled one of Father's precious bottles with buttermilk (Father had found those in the stable-yard of a great house).

He heaped all these things on the floor and put them in a newish nosebag of woven straw which he could sling over his shoulder on a leather strap.

One article remained: the only proof that he was Molly Erskine's son. Father seemed to have forgotten her little work box, and Timothy had hidden it under the thatch of his loft. He took it out now. It was only a foot square and perhaps four inches deep, made of mahogany and inlaid with a thin line of pearl with a round moon of the same material in the middle of the lid. Once it had owned a blue silk lining, with loops and pockets for all the tools of the seamstress; now this was in tatters and only a few small objects lay in a forlorn jumble. There was a reel of beeswax, six bone bobbins for lace-making, an ivory thread-holder, shaped like two willow leaves laid face to face and held by a small bar round which the thread was turned, and a small wooden cylinder, which when unscrewed revealed two needles and a bodkin. Three pages of emery to polish the needles had been rolled first in red flannel, then in worn green brocade, and tied with blue thread. The needle holder and the other tools had been crudely incised with the letters *M. E.*—Molly Erskine—and on the outside of the box an equally inexpert hand had burned in pokerwork *MOLLY ERSKINE, UPPER DOLAGHAN, FOYLESIDE*. The box contained one other item: a very fine linen tucker, edged with a deep frill of hand-made lace.

He wrapped the box in the blue neckcloth and laid it in the bottom of the bag, piling shirt and food on top of that, and covering all with the breeches. There only remained the map. He took it out of the cupboard and studied it for the hundredth time. He saw how it matched the twelve miles or so of the countryside which were the limits of his wandering, but now he realized how vaguely indicated were the distances even in County Sligo and its neighbour County Leitrim, while in Donegal only one name was given and a couple of roads. After the little corner of Donegal a long lake was shown, and this, he knew, was in County Fermanagh with the town of Enniskillen at its further end, marking the half-way stage of his proposed journey. Beside the lake there was only one note: *J.C.'s cave*.

The general drift of his direction was north-east, so he could take either the glen road, which led east, or the coast road, which led north, and slowly come on a more direct line. In spite of these practical considerations his heart dropped as he bent over the map. How little he really knew. Even the exact distance to Foyleside was vague: perhaps ninety, perhaps a hundred miles. An active lad could cover that easily in a week if all went smoothly and he had plenty of food, but suppose he got lost in the bogs, or was held up by rainstorms, or was beaten by foot-pads, or was weak with hunger . . .

A voice spoke behind him. "And what are we up to, wee fellow?" Old Mrs Kearney, Jane's grand-mother, was standing behind him. "A fine mess you make when you're left on your own. If I hadn't come in for the lend of a pickle of salt Dear knows what you'd have been up to next. The fire near out, the hens never fed, the water still in the well, and there you stand dreaming away the day like your Mama before you." She sniffed. "Where's the salt box?"

He tossed the bag into a corner, pushed the map carelessly away, and put a liberal handful of salt into the noggin she held. "Here it is. I've not done anything— You'll not be saying . . ."

"Wee boys shouldn't go prying into particulars about the house when they're left to mind it. You'll take what's coming like the rest of us." She hobbled off.

He had meant to make a big meal so that he need not eat until the next day, but Granny Kearney's visit had scared him. He snatched up his own wooden noggin to hang from his belt, tucked the map into the bag and had reached for the farmyard gate when he remembered his pocket knife and the precious ten shillings and seven pence he had saved up. He ran back and climbed into the loft to clear the niche in the wall, just above the place where Brandy and he slept. He could see the hollow his body had made in the straw, and Brandy's special place shaped like a nest. For a moment his resolution wavered. Why not stay after all? Father might relent. His new mother might be sweeter after the baby came. Old Granny Kearney might not tell tales. Running away wouldn't be so bad if he could have Jane and Brandy with him. Leaving them was like—like betraying friends as Mama said some did in the '98— Brandy would howl and pine and perhaps die. He was the only real friend Brandy had except Jane—and he'd never even said good-bye to her. If only they hadn't taken the dog with them this morning— Wandering the roads with Jane or Brandy would be fun. Without them it would feel as lonely as that curlew had sounded last night. He huddled miserably in the straw, hollow with grieving, and then suddenly, as if his mother was telling it to him, he remembered the white house above the river, and the boat and the orchard, and the kind bachelor uncle: Molly Erskine's house where he had never been, and which must now be his home. He scampered down the ladder and away to the road that ran east by the glen. He dared not think of Jane or of Brandy. He filled his mind with pictures of the place he had never seen and ran until he must sink to a jog-trot.

There was little doing on the glen road, for the coach had already passed and the fair-day traffic had gone in the opposite direction hours ago and had not yet begun the homeward journey. Timothy was at least half a mile on his way before he saw anyone, and unfortunately it was Barney Doggart the packman, who knew him well. His heart dropped, but he tried to march past with a "Good-day."

The packman had time on his hands and as much curiosity as Granny Kearney and could not fail to see the pack over the boy's shoulders. "Are you miching?" He shook his head in mock reproof. "The newly weds go off to the fair and their jack-of-all-trades takes a day off as soon as their backs are turned."

Timothy put on a bold face. "There was a heifer missing. I thought—"

"Will Maguire's fences are too good for that tale to hold water. Anyway there's nary a heifer to be seen." His twinkling little eyes held no malice. "Away home, boy."

Timothy almost took to his heels, for he could soon outdistance the bent little man, but if he did, the news of his escape and the road he had taken would soon reach his father, and what chance would he have against Will Maguire's big chestnut mare in pursuit? Without even trying he looked sulky. "It was a brave day—and feeding the stock and milking and—"

The packman took up the list. "And getting in the turfs and drawing the water and redding up the yard— Ay, boy, it's dull, but in a few years you'll be grown and able to pick and choose. There's no need to run into trouble. Come on, I'll put you to the end of the loaning and forget I ever set eyes on you. Your mother bought a grand lot of stuff in her day from me, God rest her."

He was better than his word. Not only did he walk Timothy to the farm track's end, but he slipped two pennies into his hand before nodding good-bye. "Not that I've seen you at all, mind that."

Timothy went down the lane wondering whether to laugh or to cry. Two pennies were more than welcome, but it was now after noon and he would have to start all over again by the windy coast road. He was so disgruntled that he forgot to keep out of sight of the Kearneys' cottage. Only this time it was Jane who spied him. "Timothy—" She too saw his pack and her grey eyes rounded. "What's the pack for? What are you—" She snatched him into the shadow of the turf stack. "Ssssh, she's looking for eggs."

The old woman poked into every corner of the two sheds and went into the house calling. "Jane! Dear help us, where's the child run to now?"

Jane did not answer. She said to Timothy: "Granny wondered what you were after this morning." She searched his face. "You—you're running away, aren't you? She"— they both knew who 'she' was—"she never had a notion to you, and he'll jump over the moon to please her. Take me with you. They'll never lift a finger to find out if I've run away or fallen into a boghole. Once Uncle's married next month I'll be sent out to work in any house that'll take me. No one wants me any more than *she* wants *you*. I can walk as well as a boy. I'll be no trouble to you. I'll go wherever you want: wherever it is I'll find work. I can milk and churn and stitch a hem and even spin a little—" Her voice trailed off at the expression on his face. Suddenly she looked thinner and smaller, even her crisp brown hair seemed to lose its curl. "You'll not do it. You'd rather have Brandy than me any day. You've forgotten the thrashing I saved you when the clocking hen ran off, or the other time—" With head downbent she turned, looked back at him, then clapped her hand over her mouth and ran blindly into the house.

Timothy went on to the coast road to begin his walk to Foyleside. But he could not forget her any more than he could forget Brandy. They walked invisibly beside him, their silent voices loud as bells in his ears.

Chapter Two

A COMPANION

HE THOUGHT IT was unlikely that anyone
would come in search of him until late evening.
He slogged along the rough road, between sea and
mountain, standing in gateways to look at the
cattle if he heard anyone coming, trying to be incon-
spicuous as a sparrow. But most people were at the
fair. The blind beggar, tapping his way round the
corners, never noticed him, and the two young

soldiers, back from fighting against Napoleon, were too eager to meet their sweethearts again to take any notice of a lanky boy.

The road seemed longer than he remembered it and evening was upon him before he had gone over half-way to the nearest village. There the road did not follow the indented coast but took an uphill short-cut, a bleak stretch exposed to the full force of the Atlantic winds. Here there were no houses, the clouds stooped lower, and for the first time he could see the direction he must take beyond his own townland. He had seen many times before the fall of land leading to a maze of fields and streams and woods and tiny holdings, but had never until now considered how many other such views he must see before he reached Foyleside.

Until he paused he had not known how tired and hungry he was. After all, he had not eaten since breakfast and had slept little the night before. But there could be no turning back. His father would be home by now, and was either raging round the farm, or even on the road behind him, and probably half-drunk at that. Perhaps after all, it would be safer to take a short cut over the mountainy land above the road to the right. Belatedly he climbed over the loose stone ditch. There was a stack of peats not far above, which could serve both as shelter and vantage point. By first light he would cut over the hill and if he only kept free for another day he would almost be safe, for his step-mother would see that her husband wasted little time in looking for his brat. But if only, if only Jane or Brandy were here, to warm him with their company. Jane thought him so clever and Brandy was so cosy to lie against at night.

He gritted his teeth and went up to the turf-stack, where he made a shaky kind of cave on the leeward side. This warmed him up again. He drank part of his buttermilk, gobbled an oatcake-and-butter sandwich, and had started on the next before he wondered where the day after tomorrow's rations were to come from. Sighing, he wrapped up the crumbly fragment, tucked himself into his old blanket and waited.

In the half-dark the lonely place was hostile. He had to keep looking over his shoulder to see if any-one were watching him. He had never before slept alone outside four safe walls, and realized for the first time what his father meant when in the course of an occasional prayer, he said: "Lord deliver us from the perils of darkness." This was a place and a time which belonged to the outcasts, tinkers and beggars, men escaping from justice, men who would never again know a home or sit at a hearth fire. He belonged to this wandering company now and he did not know how to deal with it or with his own terrors. He longed wholeheartedly to be back in the loft and secure in the sweet hay. He tried to pull his thoughts on to his goal, but the little house on the river bank where Molly had lived seemed very far away. Suppose it had even been pulled down, and he arrived there to find only strangers who did not know the name of Erskine? Far far off at the back of his mind a small voice muttered: "You're the son of a man brave enough to fight for his rights, and of a woman who was brave enough to hide him from the soldiers and to leave home for his sake. You know farmwork. You can hire yourself out at a fair. You can read and write—'' But the voice was very small under the darkening sky, and no matter how he wrapped himself in his blanket, his teeth chattered. He had begun to see dark forms crouching under every whin bush and to hear low voices in the wind, when a real sound struck through his fantasies: fifty feet below him a tired horse was trudging up the road and its rider was swearing in a slurred drunken voice, only too well known to Timothy. "Get on, you spavined old brute. Get on and let's be done with it."

Timothy heard the clap of a stick on the beast's hind-quarters. His father must be very drunk: he never struck the mare when sober. Now he hallooed: "Timothy! Is this the road you've taken?" The words slurred. "If you weren't Molly's brat I'd never bother my head. TIMOTHY!" His voice rose to a menacing yell. "And where's that so-and-so dog gone when he should be at my heels hunting? Why I feed him or the brat either—"

In the momentary halt a dog barked and Timothy held his breath: once Brandy got on his scent the dog could innocently betray him by bounding in welcome. As he waited, the angry man below him whacked his mare once more, and the tired beast lost patience. She whinnied and at the same time twisted and reared to rid herself of her demanding rider, for Timothy heard a ragged scrape of hooves on the road, mingled with his father's curses. Then the mare whinnied again. An oath cut off in mid-utterance rang out, something thumped loudly on to the roadside grass, and lay silent. The mare hesitated, then moved downhill.

Timothy caught his breath, listening: it was not the first time that such a thing had happened. Once his father had got up and found his own way home, once the Kearney uncle had set out to look for him. "Born to be hung," he had said as he dusted Will down. "You'll never die of a dunt on the head."

But even as these memories rushed through his mind he was out of the shelter of his turf-stack and running back to the road. He reached the fallen man just as Brandy panted up. The dog gave one sniff at Will Maguire and rushed at Timothy, licking and barking and whimpering for joy. "Hush boy, you'll have the whole countryside awakened." Despite what seemed like the end of his venture the dog's greeting put new heart into him. He forgot the lonely night and bent over his father, trying to find out what was amiss. Will was lying limply on his back, breathing as if asleep, and when Timothy gingerly tested his arms and legs they seemed quite sound. Even his head was unbroken, and as Timothy eased it to a more comfortable angle on the grass, he stirred, his eyes flickered open and he muttered something about "—missed him—" Then he gave a tremendous belch and fell into a stuporous sleep.

Immensely relieved, Timothy sat back on his heels and Brandy leant close against him, with a little grunt of satisfaction. He had always been Timothy's dog first and farm dog second and was now merely awaiting his master's orders. It was a good thing he could not see into the confusion of

Timothy's mind. He was running away, yet he could not desert his father. It was likely that the mare would reach the farm, and his step-mother would rouse the Kearneys. Help was certain, and to all appearances his father merely drunk. Even if he ran home himself he was so tired that the mare would outdistance him and bring speedier help. Yet—yet— He rubbed his head against Brandy's. He had needed Brandy so much, and now the dog had come he could not take him and go off with a clear conscience. He must wait till help came. He hugged the dog hard, swallowed down his disappointment and was faintly surprised at the steadiness of his voice as he said, "Sit boy." He scurried up to the turf-stack and brought down the blanket, wrapped it about his father, and then, huddled against the dog for warmth, sat down to watch.

In spite of the chilly air and downcast spirits he drowsed fitfully, waking now and again with a start to make sure his father really was breathing, and to chafe his rough hands. He had to stamp about too, partly to scare away nightmares and false alarms, partly to keep out the plain ordinary cold of the midnight hours. Brandy sighed in a puzzled way, and once, when a fox barked on the hillside, broke away on a vain chase. Timothy feared he would not return, but he did, glowing with excitement. Borne on the rising west wind, sounds of men's voices floated up from below. Timothy sprang to his feet. "Sssh Brandy, wait boy." If the men had dogs with them, Brandy could betray them both.

The shouting was replaced by a double plod-plod.

That could be that poor mare again, and perhaps the Kearneys' ass. It seemed to take a long time before Timothy saw the flicker of a lamp on the last slope of the hill. He snatched his blanket up, turned to run, checked in mid-stride and waited until the men, whoever they were, had reached the level stretch at the head of the road. They were approaching on the left-hand side where his father lay and just before the glimmer of the lamp could fall on him he hooked his fingers firmly into Brandy's pelt and, whispering "Sssh Brandy," went through the gap in the stone ditch and uphill as fast as he could, praying that the wind would drown the noise of their footsteps. Once, Brandy whimpered with excitement, and he had to stop and clamp his hands about the dog's muzzle. At least the men below did not seem to have the dogs with them, so there was still a hope that they might escape undetected. With the dog he reached the shelter of the turf-stack and waited, praying that the men would see the fallen figure.

They did not pass on. An instant later he recognized Jane's uncle's voice shouting. "He's here. The mare's throwed him." Followed a few minutes of fumbling and lifting. "Ay, he's none the worse, but for the drink. Come morning he'd be fit to bring himself down the road."

"You'd not want the weight of her tongue on your shoulders, now would you?"

The other chuckled. "What d'you think brung me up the glen? Heth, it was never love of Will!"

With many grunts they heaved him up on the donkey. The little beast brayed in some kind of

protest, and a moment later all of them set off down
the road again. He loosened his hold on Brandy.
The dog whimpered, uncertain where his duty lay,
then, as the hoofbeats died away, and Timothy
drew him closer, yawned into the boy's face. It was
a broad hint. Timothy was by now so tired that he
could think and plan no more. They dropped asleep
together, not even stirring when some of the peats
in the stack were dislodged by the wind and fell on
the edge of the blanket.

Dawn awakened them. Up here it was clear, in
the lands below every watercourse was veiled by
mist. He made a chilly breakfast of the remains of
the buttermilk and one hard-boiled egg. The broken
oatcake was the dog's share. If he needed more, he
would hunt. How lucky that he had been littered on
a gentleman's estate. Timothy wished belatedly
that he had brought flint and tinder with him. A
dog could stomach raw rabbit better than could
his master.

He cast a last look behind him and walked on
towards the other home which he had seen only in
dream and story.

This time he kept on the rough ground high
above the road which now turned inland. He was
not yet frightened of losing his way, for he had been
often to the next village, Ballydoran, on fair days,
and indeed, had better steer clear of it lest he be
recognized as a cattle drover's son.

Brandy had no fears of being recognized. A
few minutes later he startled a hare, and went in
chase, his barks echoing from hillside to hillside.
The noise was worth it, for, as he had been trained,

he came back carrying the carcase. Timothy cut it at the lower ribs and gave the dog his customary share, the front quarters. Remained the best half: if only he was far away from possible acquaintances, he would beg a light at a cottage fire, and roast his dinner and supper and next breakfast. His mouth watered at the thought, and as he stood wondering what to do a whiff of wood smoke drifted up to him. It was well screened by high thorns, but seemed to come from the corner of a field at the triple lane-ends. Several asses, moving awkwardly, as if hobbled, had come up on the outside of the hedge to join the tethered goats, and when he peered closely he could glimpse the shape of a rickety cart, and a ragged scatter of colour, possibly garments spread out to dry tinker-fashion. He could get fire there.

Without thinking of tinkers' dogs and their traditional mistrust of strangers, he trotted downhill, only stopping to gather some sturdy whin branches topped with prickles; even when green these would flare quickly into a splendid fire. He was already on the verge of the road when the dogs in the encampment began to fight. Brandy must be kept in check, and by nothing else than leather too. Timothy crouched behind a bank and used the few materials to hand. His belt could become Brandy's lead and the twine in the neck of the bag could replace his belt. He contrived all this, and picked up his burdens once more. Then he squeezed through a gap in the tinkers' hedge.

The two dogs broke off their fight and ran silently to meet him, and a group of tinkers—a young man and an ancient, a woman and a handful of children—stared stonily at him from where they squatted about the fire. They were quite the most ragged crew he had ever seen, and he searched in vain for a friendly face. These were the outcasts of whom he had dreamed during his uneasy night on the hillside.

"And what might you be after?" said the younger man, a tawny-haired fellow, one of whose shoulders was higher than the other which gave a menacing look, as if he were already moving forward to attack. "Is it a kettle you want mended?"

"Or your fortune told?" The woman smiled at him, then blew her nose between her fingers and wiped them on her dirty skirts. "Or maybe you're after clothes pegs?" She scooped some out of her pocket and held them out on her grimy hand. "Has the cat got your tongue? Where's the colour of you ha'pence?"

They rose smoothly as if they had been drilled and closed in, eyeing his dog, his well-filled bag, the newly-killed hare. Too late Timothy realized he should have left his load behind the bushes: to these vagrants his pack spelled all the goods they must do without—or take by craft or force.

The man reached out and would have snatched the bag had not Brandy leapt, narrowly missing his wrist. He backed, and again, as if to a signal, the other circled round, shutting out Timothy's retreat.

He pretended nothing was amiss. "I only wanted to get a light from your fire."

The man laughed. "Fire's riches, not easy got nor easy given. What'll you pay for it?"

"The—the kindling." And as the man shook his head—"Half the forequarters of the hare."

"It takes more than that to feed my litter. What's in the pack? Maybe we'd be cooking the hare in the pot and you'd get a share—if—" He grinned, showing teeth as brown as dead tree stumps—"If you were sharing what's in thon pack first."

The woman edged nearer. "Think about it, son, you've a dog, but we've two. You're just a thin slip of a lad and there's six of us."

The man added, "When you've your belly full with what's in the pot it'll be tight as a drum." He smacked his lips. "My woman here's the best hand with a stew that ever you met since you were weaned—she'd not last long here if she wasn't, would you, girl?"

All the false geniality dropped from her face. "Stop your gabbing and get him. All mouth and no do, that's the kind of man you are. Even the childer's quicker nor you."

Indeed they were already across the gap in the hedge, and Brandy had all he could do keeping the two thin curs at snapping distance. Timothy was hemmed in, and all because of his own folly. He gripped the longest branch of whin, still topped by its formidable prickles, and swung it in a wide circle about him. One of the children squealed, the dogs yelped and even the tall man ducked as the thorns grazed his chin, but the woman caught a flaming brand out of the fire and threw it full at Timothy. Its hot breath scorched one cheek and in falling touched the tip of Brandy's ear. That was too much. Timothy could no longer restrain him and was dragged straight towards the offender by the snarling dog. The children scattered, the woman tripped on her ragged petticoats and lay howling, the man ran cursing to her rescue and the old man, inactive until now, thrust out his stick in Timothy's way, as he was dragged past. Timothy lost his balance and the two dogs made for him as he fell forward.

A voice beyond the hedge cried: "The asses—the hobbles are off and they're away down the road—" The voice rose to a panic-stricken yell. "The coach is at the corner, they'll be on it in a minute, and the goats with them—they'll be slaughtered so they will—h—h—" There was a light patter of feet as of someone going in chase, and a donkey's voice up-raised in pained surprise.

The two dogs left Timothy, and the two men and the woman dived through different holes in the hedge like driven birds. The children, left on their own, made for the unguarded black pot beside the fire and began to stuff themselves.

As if by magic Brandy's hackles smoothed down, and his tongue lolled out as if he smiled while waiting for the next bit of excitement.

Timothy picked himself up. He still held his pack and the meat and one end of Brandy's lead. Only the firewood had been scattered.

"Are you clean astray in the head!" Jane Kearney squeezed through the misused hedge. "Run for it. They'll be back like redshanks when they see there's no coach at all." She pulled at his hand. Too astounded for questions he let her drag him forward, but the smell which arose from the pot was too

much for him. He unhooked the noggin at his belt
and scooped out a generous helping.

Leaving the children agape they went back to
the road and then quickly uphill towards the shelter
of the bank of whins. A cloud of finches rose twit-
tering from it and Brandy bounded forward, making
puppy-like leaps in the air at the little birds. The
whole affair of the tinkers seemed to have put him
in good humour and he was back wagging his tail
beside Jane and looking up at her before she said:
"We'll never get the hare cooked now, Timothy.
Give it to the creature, you'd not have come off so
lightly but for him." Timothy did as he was told
and turned back to her. "Where did you spring
from?"

Jane wanted to hug her little secret longer. "Sup
up your share of the broth while there's heat in it,
and then—"

They had always shared the small treats which
came their way, so he took a scrupulous two gulps
from the noggin and then passed it over to her. It
tasted different from Mother's hare soup, stronger
flavoured and slightly smoky. They licked their lips
and wished it were four times as much. Timothy
took out another piece of oatcake. "That's all for a
wee while. And now will you be telling me how you
were behind the hedge just when Brandy and I
were at our wits' end."

"We'll talk as we go. I'd like to put a mile or two
between us and the tinkers—listen to the carry-on
below there." Indeed the wind bore to them the
cries of the pursuing tinkers and the brays of the
asses. "Come on—quick!"

They left the dog to finish his meat and hurried along the mountainside, keeping well down behind the whins, whose rusty seed-pods burst as the children brushed past. Below, the sound of hoofs and voices grew fainter: it did not seem that there was going to be any pursuit. Timothy sat down on the sunny grass. "Now Jane, I thought there wasn't a soul in the townland knew where I was going. I'd put Barney Doggart off the scent and I'd dodged Papa and your uncle—but here you are."

Jane gave a superior smile. "You never went a step I didn't know it. I saw when your father came with Brandy, and I saw how you waited while the mare went back and Uncle came, and how now and then you'd drop off to sleep. Oh, it was the longest night! I was propping my eyes open with my fingers for fear I'd miss you. And then you went along the hill and I went on the road, jouking into the hedges when anyone came along." She smiled at him. "I saw you go into the tinkers' field, it was all I could do not to shout. Of all the daft ploys, Timothy, that was the daftest."

He nodded, acknowledging his debt. "But what about you? Aren't they dragging the ditches for you?"

Her grey eyes danced. "It was the luckiest thing." She cast a sidelong glance at Timothy. "Wouldn't it just be the evening when the McDonnells' great hound had got into the shed where Granny keeps her butter— If you'd seen it! Anyway, there was only the tiniest scrape left for Uncle, so Granny was sending me off hot foot up the glen to beg or borrow some. But if it came full dark I was to stay

the night with the Brownes. So no one will think of
me till mid-day." She looked gravely at him. "It
couldn't have fallen out better, now could it?"

"Not if you'd imagined the whole ploy—or
dragged in the great hound by the scruff of his neck
to make sure he saw all the butter—" He flung himself back on the bank. They rolled there, helpless
with mirth. "Mind you," said Jane, "I couldn't but
be s-sorry for G-Granny—"

When they had sobered up Timothy said: "But
wha' do we do *now*?" He looked at her, her shawl,
her work-worn gown, her thin bare feet, her
scratched hands, and then back to her hopeful face.
"You're a girl. It's different for a boy on the roads.
There's rough men and footpads—"

"And tinkers," said Jane slyly. "A girl is just as
clever in besting a tinker màn as any lad."

Timothy had no reply to that. He thought back
to the lonely night. No doubt of it, a companion
like Jane could make all the difference. "But what'll
you do?"

"I'll go on with you. I can herd the cows and
milk them and churn. I can cook and darn and sew.
I can set potatoes as well as any lad, and look after
fowl. One of the well-to-do farmers on the other
side of Sligo was asking my uncle only the other day
if he'd take me to the hiring fair—and he's a man
who owns his land."

"So does my uncle on Foyleside—I think."

"Then let's be going to him. I'll not be a charge
on anyone. Oh Timothy, aren't you telling me he'd
a boat of his own, and meat twice a week, and how
your mother never went barefoot and had two

woollen dresses? And a delft teapot with a rosebud on the lid?"

Indeed he had told her all this. Living was better on Foyleside than near Sligo, and neither of them left either love or prospects behind them. In a last effort—for it was his dream, not hers—he spread out the inky tattered map. "It's a wheen of miles. As far as we've gone ten times over, or more if we lose the way or go round the bogs and the loughs. Look!" He showed her the twisting roads, the mountains and bogland.

"We've tongues in our heads to ask the way. We can sleep in barns—how much worse is that than the places we've been sleeping in all our lives? And maybe we could be gathering turfs or making hay and sit down to potatoes and buttermilk with the rest of the family afterwards—as often and often has happened in our houses. Och Timothy, you know it has. Not a July goes by but men and girls and boys come asking for work."

He hesitated. She sighed and played her last card. Slowly she drew a linen bag from the placket of her skirt. "There's potato farls and good bacon enough for two days in that. And I've the twenty-five shillings Papa left me before he went to. fight with the Inniskilling Dragoons, in foreign places against Napoleon. Only now he's dead like your Mama." She burst into wild tears. "If—if I'm not to go with you I'll go on my lone, and if no one hires me I'll wander the roads all my life long." She hid her face in her hands and rocked back and fro in misery. Brandy licked her fingers. Her sobs broke. "Oh Brandy, you tickle so!"

Timothy folded up his map. Why must girls always pipe their eyes? But she would be safer with him, no doubt about that. The only trouble was that two children were more than twice as conspicuous as one. (And, said his sense of fairness, two can fight against tinkers better than one.) He said gruffly: "We'd best be going. The further we get from the tinkers and Ballydoran today the better, and we'll keep off the main road till we're sure Barney Doggart's well on his way in front. He'd give us up before you could say 'snipe' if he thought he'd gain a penny by it."

She sprang to her feet and hugged him. So they wandered along the mountainside, relishing the first day they had ever known in which they could do exactly what they chose when they chose. They did not spare a pang of conscience for what the Maguires and Kearneys might be thinking. For now all that part of their life was over and they were arrowing towards the new goal which they had chosen.

Chapter Three

BRIDIE'S LETTER

EXHILARATION CARRIED THEM on until afternoon, but long before nightfall they were heavy-eyed with lack of sleep and looked about them for shelter. Not far away among a clump of wind-blown rowans near a rocky watercourse was a half-ruined croft, and a hundred yards below that a farm. Blue turf smoke rose from its chimney, hens cackled, a very small baby set up a hungry howl and a woman, presumably its mother, hastened across the yard towards the house. Her gay call rose clearly to them as she entered. "Hush, you wee ruffian!" She laughed, and the rest was lost to the listeners though Jane thought she could hear the baby chuckle and the woman murmur a lullaby. She would soon have it in her arms on the low stool beside the hearth.

Without thinking Jane said: "Granny would have the pot on for supper about now."

Timothy had a vision of his father's hearth and his stepmother bustling about it: even with her there that kitchen was cosier than this deserted croft. He said slowly, "You could still go back if you wanted, I'd be seeing you safe on the road."

She shook her head. "Didn't you tell me there was always a fire burning in the house on Foyleside?" Without another look at the little self-sufficient community below them, she went into the ruinous building.

A heap of last year's fodder lay in the far corner, where the roof gave tolerable shelter. She curled up like a sleepy cat on it, drawing her shawl about her. "You'd best tether Brandy—" Her voice trailed off in a yawn. Soon Timothy joined her and they slept. Brandy was more wakeful than they. He heard geese fly over during the night, heading for Fermanagh and the lake, growled at some wandering predator, and some time in the dawn, eased his lead out of Timothy's slack hand and went off. A little later a hen squawked in the farmyard below, and in an instant the place was in commotion. The first the children knew of it was when Brandy bounded in, his muzzle covered in blood and small white feathers. He must have pounced on a pullet and torn it to pieces.

Timothy secured his lead and shook Jane awake. "They'll think the fox has broken in and have a dog out after him. Quick—" Jane rubbed the sleep out of her eyes. "Where'll we go?"

He peered through the opening which had once been a window. The farm was belatedly astir now and—yes—a dog had begun to bark. He gripped Brandy close before the dog could issue a challenge. "If we went down by the stream, bent double, the banks'ld hide us. Once we're on the road we can run. They'll never seek a fox there."

They hurried, bruising their toes on dry rocks, luxuriating an instant in the sandy silt brought down by floodwater. By the time they reached the road the farm dog was making for the croft: at least Brandy had been cunning enough to make a detour. Where the stream flowed across the road, Timothy halted, and while Jane got two hard-boiled eggs from his pack and added to them the last of her potato bread, he forced Brandy to stand in the deepest pool and sluiced him down. The dog repaid him by waiting until his master had turned to receive his breakfast from Jane, and then shaking his coat dry over them.

They hurried down the lane, and came on to the main road. It would be much easier to follow that than to draw attention to themselves by asking the way, or by depending on their very vague map. But they were still too near the little town of Ballydoran above which the tinkers had camped. Tomorrow they could risk it. Without even a consultation, they crossed the road quietly as hares, and began to thread their way through a maze of lanes. Four turnings later and they were as good as lost.

"We must try to keep as near the coach road and the river as we can," said Timothy, "that way we'll get through the tail of Leitrim and Donegal, and after a mile or two we'll reach Fermanagh and we'll have the big lake to guide us. That'll be half way."

"However do you know all that?"

"Mama came this way when they were running from the soldiers after the '98. Uncle Alexander has more than a bit of book-learning so he'd the teaching of her. That's how she came to be able to make a map and read a book."

Jane's face fell. "I've never seen any map but this, and though Granny's after keeping a book or two in the press they'd hardly ever be out. I can only read the little wee words. What'll your uncle say to the likes of that?"

"He'll never worry his head," said Timothy.

Soon the tail of the mountain was behind them, and all that day they walked along narrow tracks. The blue hills which rimmed the horizon were too distant to be of any help as landmarks, and soon the coach road and the river were lost behind coppices and wrinkles of ground. No hill was big enough to afford a clear view, and there were few farms and few passers-by.

This was foothill country. Most of it had never known the plough and was overgrown by whins and brambles and rushes, among which a goat or two and small black cattle grazed forlornly, accompanied by an ass or pinioned geese. Living had always been hard here, and shells of cottages showed how families had left for the towns where their menfolk could earn more money by becoming labourers or even by joining the army. The lucky few saved enough to emigrate to England or America where work was plentiful and food was cheap. (One of the Kearneys had done that, along with Will Maguire's elder brother.) To farmers' children such as Jane and Timothy, it was a sad countryside. To a land-owner, it could be a paradise, for it was rich in duck and geese, snipe and wood pigeons, hares and rabbits. There was no lack of foxes to be hunted, and even a few pheasants and deer.

A poacher could live well here, but tinkers and beggars lacked householders from whom to seek alms, while footpads and highwaymen only came if they wished to hide until trouble blew over.

At first Jane and Timothy walked on happily enough. Of course, they talked incessantly of the Foyleside haven as pictured and preached by Molly Erskine. "No beggar is ever sent from their door," said Timothy. "Mama said that they'd take meat from their own pot to feed a stranger if he was hungry. They'd shoes to wear, and even children had a straw palliasse to lie on or maybe a crib, and when they were nearly grown, they'd a wee room to themselves—not just the loft with the turf reek in it and mice among the hay."

Jane prompted him. "There was a parlour too for Sundays—"

"And a table with a cloth on it for holidays. And a great big lustre jug, shining like copper, sitting on

the mantelshelf by the sampler that Great Grandmother was after making in cross-stitch to show she
knew her 'A.B.C.' "

"Granny can do the cross-stitch," said Jane.

But Timothy had more to say. "And under the
A.B.C. part she'd made real words—" He found a
stick and laboriously wrote them on a sandy piece
at the side of the road. "*Lord bless this house.*"

"That's what every beggar at the door says—
bless the house."

"But this was written down in coloured stitchery.
That makes it seem special."

Jane agreed that it did. Blues and reds and greens
were much more interesting than the thick blurry
lettering in Granny's two tattered books.

So ran the talk, helping their legs to forget the
miles, though it did little to stay the rumblings of
their half-filled stomachs. Eggs and scraps of
Timothy's indifferently cooked ham and oatcake
fragments were all very well, but they could not
begin to fill the gap usually taken up by big bowls
of porridge, and as many potatoes and noggins of
buttermilk as they could swallow.

Gradually the sun clouded over. Their tongues
and legs slowed. Even Brandy's early high spirits
flagged. He kept running forward, and coming
back to gaze anxiously up at them, as if alarmed by
some invisible danger. Jane seemed to voice his
feelings when she said: "It was nicer yesterday
among the whins. Hereabouts you might be walking
in a fog for all you can see."

"Maybe round the next corner—" He did not
finish. The next bend revealed merely a new wind-

ing track, bordered by scrub and derelict boggy
land. Timothy could not help wondering why the
lane had ever been made. Still, they could not be
far out in their reckoning, for they had steered by
the sun all morning and the far blue hills had grown
less like clouds and more like solid land— But no,
they had quietly been swallowed by the feathery
grey clouds which were creeping up the sky. Without the far horizon, the place seemed lonelier than
ever.

However, the next corner but one revealed
something different. They almost bumped into a
ragged boy about their own age. He looked even
hungrier than they felt, his cheeks were hollow, his
thin shoulders poked through his home-spun jacket,
and—Brandy growled at this—his big-knuckled
hands were tight on the limp body of a rabbit. At
the sight of them he would have run, had not
Timothy caught his tattered sleeve. "We'll not
hurt you. Where's this lane leading, and where's
the coach road?"

The boy stuttered incomprehensible words. Jane
broke in. "He only has the Irish. Let me. I can get
my tongue round it better than you." She repeated
the questions.

The lad answered briefly, pointed down the road,
thrust the rabbit inside his coat and jerked himself
free. He was over the rickle of stones that bordered
the lane and away before Brandy could growl a
second time.

"He says the lane meets the coach road four
miles on."

"Nothing about a house?"

"I'd not the time to ask him." She sighed—
"Sure any place he came from wouldn't have food
enough to feed a banshee." She clapped a hand
over her mouth. "Oh what'd I say a thing like that
for? It's that kind of place." She sketched a curtsey
and said in a hurried gabble, "Fair may you come
and fair may you go—and our backs to you."

Timothy said in tones which lacked all conviction,
"Papa says that banshees and the like are just old
women's gabble."

"Never mind what he says. Don't you utter one
single word about them—or I'll away and leave
you. It's not safe, so it's not. Be talking about—"
She searched desperately for something safe and
ordinary. "About the dresser in your mama's
kitchen, the blue delft on it and the teapot and—
and—"

The first of the rain spattered among the hazels
as Timothy racked his brains. "Well now, one of the
bowls had a crack in it and a chip out of the side,
and one day a tinker's child came whining to the
door for a bite and sup for her wee sick sister—"

The loss of the bowl kept them going for a few
minutes, but bowls make one think of food, and
they were on the very last of their rations now.

Silently they hurried on, full into the downpour.
Brandy kept on the leeward side of Jane, sheltering
from the rain. Long before they reached the boy's
promised coach road they found four cocks of
rushy hay near a little coppice. Surely a farm must
be near. They looked in vain through the mist for
a trail of smoke or a glimmer of white walls. Deep
among the trees which clustered by the stream there

well might be a house, but suddenly even another half-mile seemed too much. "We could g-get w-warm in the hay," said Jane through chattering teeth.

They made little caves for themselves and Brandy, and settled down to wait it out. Three eggs and one potato farl was all that remained of their rations. They kept the farl for the morning and divided the eggs between the three of them but because Brandy could hunt and they could not, he only got one tiny slice from each egg, which was a tremendous sacrifice. He gave a doggy sigh and trotted off. He did not return for some time, and they had begun to worry when he trotted jauntily back, licking his whiskers. "I wish I was a dog and could hunt," said Timothy crossly. "Get into the hay and be warm, you greedy creature, you!"

They had hardly got under cover before they heard their first horseman of the day coming at a furious pace. Timothy clapped his hand on Brandy's muzzle, Jane clenched her teeth on a scream which was trying to climb up her throat.

He swept past, a tall dark man on a chestnut mare. She had gone lame, and he was lashing at her flanks with an ashplant. The smell of his anger hung in the air behind him. No one who had ever seen Will Maguire in a rage could mistake him.

When all sound had disappeared Timothy whispered: "We've only to lie hidden tonight to be safe, he'll turn for home soon. The mare's too lame to carry him. He"—in spite of himself his voice shook—"he's a liking for the mare—it's only when he's a black rage on him—"

"I know." Jane spoke through chattering teeth. She crawled out of her cave and crept in to share Timothy's. "It's a whispery sort of place. Don't you hear noises in it even when—when he's gone?"

"Sure, that's only the stream rising." Timothy was not comfortable enough to be able to hearten his chilly companion. At that moment Foyleside was so far off as to be no use at all.

"There's a twinkly sort of light too. Like the kind the—the"—she slipped into the Irish word for the fairy people—"the *Sidhe* would be having to lead you into a bog hole so's you'd never be found again."

"You're astray in your head. It's a farmhouse sure as your Granny's got grey geese. If it's not I— I'll give you an extra bite of farl in the morning."

"Potato farls fresh from the griddle and they with butter on them," whispered Jane. "I could be eating a dozen this very minute."

In the thought of them she forgot her fears and presently Brandy squeezed in beside them. His pelt was wet and rank, but very warm, and slowly they stopped shivering. Belatedly Jane remembered the prayers that Granny had taught her and said as many of them as she could remember. The familiar words soothed her until she fell into a confusion of dreams.

When they awakened rain was still falling. They ate the last potato farl in three bites, and considered. "Maybe it'll be clearing soon."

So they waited. And waited. No matter how they burrowed into their haycocks they still were chilly. Even Brandy failed to flush any game and returned to skulk in the shelter of Jane's skirt, rain dripping from every tawny hair. It must have been well past mid-day when they could endure it no longer and trailed desolately downhill above the noisy stream, now brown with mud and bog drainings from the mountain country in which it had been born.

At the second bend of the road Timothy exclaimed: "There's your bog-lights for you!"

Across the stream, tucked well into a dense little covert, was a two-roomed cabin. Hens clustered against the more sheltered gable, a goat nickered from the shed, and turf smoke wafted across to them mingled with the less pleasant odour of a great dunghill on the low side of the wet yard, where stepping stones had been laid amongst the puddles. Jane slipped her cold hand into Timothy's. "Quick, let's go."

"Likely they'll hardly have enough for themselves." He sniffed the turf reek longingly. "If we gave them one of my pennies they'd not refuse to let us dry ourselves by the fire and have a sup of buttermilk and a potato or so—"

"Or oatcake. Or maybe an egg."

By a miracle they remembered to fish out a penny from the bottom of the sack and to put Brandy on his lead before they ran downhill, their legs still shaky with cold and hunger.

Yet when they came to the half-door they did not know what to say. They had seen many and many a beggar, but they had never begged.

"You knock," whispered Timothy.

"No, you be doing it. You're the biggest."

Timothy tried twice before his knuckles rapped smartly on the wood, and then, when the young woman came forward, he did not know what to say. She clicked her tongue. "Sure, you're foundered. Where under the shining sun have you been? Come away in to the fire." She bustled them forward. "You've got the dog well-trained anyways. He'll keep off a wheen of robbers. But what's brought you into these parts? We wouldn't see a strange face in a month of Sundays."

Timothy hesitated and then said: "We're going to my uncle—he's a farm on Foyleside."

"That'll be in the black north. They do say there's better living in them parts." She shrugged. "If there's such a thing as a fat living off Irish land." She looked them up and down as they steamed and shivered by the fire. "Dear help you. You're as lean as the rest of us."

The pot slung over the fire began to bubble and to send out thin steam, not so rich as that of the tinkers' stew, but good enough to make the wanderers' mouth water. The woman bent to stir it, looked over her shoulder at them and then down at the two young children who had come out of the inner room and now stood gaping at the strangers. They could almost see her mind at work. "Is there enough in the pot for us all?" Slowly she went to the meal chest, took out a scant handful and scattered it into the broth adding a more liberal amount of water. As she went to the creel of potatoes Timothy said: "We could be paying for praties and a wee drink of buttermilk. We're not wishful to take it from the childer. I've—I've two pennies here."

She shook her head. "It'll be a poor day when I can't feed a couple of children all alone in this God-forsaken back of nowhere." But her face brightened and the potatoes were peeled and tossed into the pot with an energy quite lacking in the careful distribution of the meal. "This is only a loop road, and not one on it has two ha'pence to rub together. Why weren't you on the coach road? There's company on it, and shelter, even if it's only in a loft."

Jane turned about to dry the front of her skirt. "There—there was a terrible crowd of tinkers." Not wishing to enlarge on the subject she sought a diversion and her glance fell on a folded piece of paper on the mantelshelf. It had a broken blob of sealing wax on it, and even her eye, little skilled in reading, could see that the straggling letters were an address. "Even if you're away from the coach road the carrier or packman must come by."

Bright colour ran into the woman's thin cheeks and ebbed as quickly. "It was Barney Doggart the packman brung it. I've had nary a word these two years past from my man Peter and"—she wrung her hands in exasperation—"and Barney could've read it easy enough but I wasn't wanting him to poke his nose in, and I've not seen hilt nor hair of the priest all week. There was a man came to the door yesterday at the worst of the rain—" She broke off, looking slantwise at them. More slowly she added: "But I'd never have asked him to read the letter."

"Why not?" asked Jane.

"The way he carried on—and me alone—as if he owned the place. Had I seen that one and had I seen the other, and what was that hidden at the bottom of the hay? Well for you I says, that Peter's not here or—"

Timothy sprang up, hand on his pack, ready for flight. "What was he like?"

"Well, he wasn't John Capple the highwayman anyways, for *he's* thickset and always grinning to himself, and his horse is black as pitch. This was a tall dark fellow with a great beard and eyes wild as fire. Riding a chestnut mare that'd gone lame. He'd scoured the coach road as far as Beleady and was looking through the lanes as a last hope."

"And who was he looking for?"

"A lad who'd run off, though little he liked him by his manner of talking. A right rascal he said— though I'd believe the Devil himself before I'd believe him. He said there was a girl away too— though not his kin—"

She pointed: "You're the boy. Aren't you? You"—her finger turned to Jane—"you're the girl. Now what's all the fussation about? Just be telling me that afore we go any further."

Hesitatingly at first, and then in a rush, they told her of their situation at home. "So we're making for my uncle and he'll give us shelter till we can be working. But if you'd rather see the back of us—"

She rose and pushed Timothy gently into his seat. "Sit you quiet, child. You're of gentle kind. He never was and never could be. He's away now and you're as safe as when your mother was carrying you. I'd not blame you, it's ill living where there's no love."

Timothy began to feel warm again. She smiled reassuringly at him and took up her tale. "The long and the short of it is the letter is lying here, and not a body to read it, for all the schooling I ever had would lie in a hen's eye. I've near worn my knees out praying that it's from Peter himself."

"Wouldn't you know the writing?"

"Child dear, when Peter went off to the city without as much as a by-your-leave he didn't know a B from a bullsfoot, so—so—" As Timothy bent forward to pick up the paper she exclaimed: "You've the cut of a scholar!"

"He can read books and letters and maps," said Jane

"Well, tell me the name at the foot of it then. I've stared at it till I was near blind. Is it—" she swallowed. "What is it?"

Timothy puzzled over the smudged writing, which had been done with a ragged quill in an unpractised hand and was now blotted by rain and further blurred by much folding and unfolding.

"It looks like '*Yure loveing husband Petter*'—no, Peter—and then there's a big X."

She sank to the floor as if her legs had given way under her. "Saints be praised. He's alive. He's not forgotten us. What's in the rest of it? You're doing bravely."

With much stammering and hesitation, he read it through.

"*My dere Wife Bridie my workmate writes for me as I can only make my mark yet but maybe our childer will do*

*better nor me. Enough of that how are you and Paudeen and
Mary. There is Work aplenty here on the roads but
Lodgings is bad and never a taste of broth like yours. But
Bridie I have Money saved and please God we will be
under the same roof again. Michael says his hand is wore
out with all the writing so I'll be telling you all when I
come and that'll be soon. So have all ready for comming to
Dublin with yure loveing husband Peter. X."*

"Jesus, Mary and Joseph," she murmured. "It's
all like the priest said: after the trial you'll get your
reward. Peter will be with us again. No more long
nights wondering if the roof will stand the weather,
setting potatoes, haggling for a pickle of meal with
the dealer, wondering how long before the cow goes
dry and the childer start whinging because their
bellies are sore with hunger—" She sprang up.
"Never heed the pennies. We'll be eating well the
night if it's the last thing I do afore Peter walks in
the door."

She bustled round, fetching out boxty bread and
a slab of oily butter, chopping off pieces from the
scant remains of a side of bacon, which she put to
simmer in the pot, pouring noggins of buttermilk
with a lavish hand. Soon even Brandy had a dish
of broth to lap, and the rest of them were at the
table. Before she began to feed Paudeen and Mary
she saw that the two visitors had the best of the
bacon-and-broth and thick slabs of boxty bread and
butter to go with it.

As she fed them she talked, like a river which has
been frozen and now feels the touch of a belated
spring. What Peter had done. What Peter would do.
How happily they would live in Dublin. How the

children would get schooling and how she would sell the cow and fowls at a profit—

Jane and Timothy let the words spill over them. When the meal was over they sat back, half asleep, full and warm and contented as house cats in a lord's household. The world already seemed a different place. Now they knew that all would go well and they would reach Foyleside.

"It's a sign," thought Jane, stretching lazily in the blessed warmth. "Things coming right for her is a sign for us." She smiled at Bridie, and bent down to talk to Mary and Paudeen. Soon she was singing riddles to them, and they were laughing and cuddling close to her, as once she and Timothy had clung about Molly Erskine.

Bridie watched. "It's long and long since we've had singing here. Can you not show us a jig-step?" So Jane lifted her drab skirts and jigged in the fire glow on the earthen floor. Presently Timothy joined her and their shadows tangled on the ceiling while Bridie hummed and clapped her hands to keep the time. Brandy caught the infection and pranced round too, until everyone was out of breath and must come to a panting laughing halt.

Jane sat down with the two children nestling beside her. She thought how happy it would be to have a family, and a fire to warm them by and food in the press to give them. Maybe in Foyleside— maybe—maybe—

Opposite her Bridie also had her dreams, as she caressed the letter between her hands as if it were a live thing, the touch of which brought comfort. Presently, however, she rose, put more potatoes and bacon trimmings into the pot for the morning's meal, and made up the fire. Afterwards she bundled the children to bed, the two small ones in the top of the box bed, and Jane and Timothy at the foot. "I'll sit and watch, for I'll never sleep the night for thinking of Peter and the brave days in front of us."

Soon all the children slept. The fire lighted Bridie's worn dreaming face, and burnished Brandy's rough pelt to bronze. Presently he wriggled closer, lay on the edge of her skirts and slept too. If any banshee howled that night, no one heard her. No place in the country could have been happier or more peaceful than Bridie's cottage.

Chapter Four

STRANGERS ON THE ROAD

NEXT MORNING THE sun was shining between chinks of cloud. After they had breakfasted on the potato stew, Bridie gave them clear directions how to reach the coach road, and stocked them up with boxty bread and scraps of bacon, parcelled in Timothy's linen cloth, along with a couple of eggs and the bottle refilled with buttermilk. When he tendered her the pennies she refused to take them.

"When you were reading me the letter you paid for all. The place feels like a home again now that Peter's coming. Think of it, him seeing how big the two childer have grown." Her face was alight with expectation.

Jane exclaimed, "We'd have foundered but for you. We'll remember it all in Foyleside time and time again."

"And I'll be remembering you when we're in Dublin." She bade them good-bye, the children hanging on her skirts, the hopeful smile still lifting the corners of her mouth.

Before they had gone more than a dozen steps Jane looked back. It came to her that if Bridie's Peter returned and all the family left for the town, this cottage would soon fall into ruin like the croft where they had spent their first night together. She broke away from Timothy, ran back and kissed Bridie, tears wet on her cheeks. She hardly dared to put her feelings into words: there were so many empty cabins, suppose the Foyleside house had also lost its tenant? "Oh Bridie—" She clung to her as she had never clung to her grandmother, and went back to Timothy.

He did not seem to notice her tears. "We're well on the way now. Once on the coach road and we'll go like greyhounds." Glancing sideways at her he added: "Uncle's house on Foyleside is much bigger than Bridie's and he's got half a dozen cows, not just one poor moilie. You're not—not sorry you're coming?"

"Oh no." She gave a watery smile. "If your uncle is only half as welcoming as Bridie that's all that's needed."

Timothy was quite sure of that. He broke into a whistle, and they stepped jauntily out for the coach road.

It seemed like coming into another world to ford the stream, climb up the shingly track and stand once more on a well-made road, which looked as if it were the way to towns of importance and dignity. Timothy glanced back at Bridie's loaning. "That's a place you would easily get lost in, but—oh look—" He pointed. "A milestone. At the corner."

They ran to it "Thirteen miles to Beleady. Ten from Ballydoran," read Timothy. He pulled out his map. "Look Jane, if that's where we started, then this is where we've got to and that's where we're going. First by the lake—that's it—and then north—there."

Jane looked at it doubtfully. She lacked the scholarship to be able to translate the miles she had walked into the symbols on a piece of tattered paper. "If that's where we're heading why'd your Mama put in that wee scribble beyond there, right on the edge?" She pointed to a name on the very verge of the map.

"Tullynagardy," read Timothy. He frowned. "I'm not sure if she didn't once talk of some cousins there. It's no matter to us."

He put the map away and they went on, Brandy scampering about him as his fancy led. Indeed, it was his enthusiasm which almost betrayed them. They had halted to eat what Jane termed "Just the tiniest 'nym' of bacon," and when their own foot-steps stopped heard behind them on the road a regular tap-tap, tap-tap, punctuated with a scraping noise as if something was being trailed over the stones. Presently the noise stopped and in its place came the lilt of a fiddle playing a jig tune. "If only we'd had it last night," said Jane. "He's playing it as well as—"

Before she finished the sentence Brandy scented the player, and turned back to welcome what was to him a well-known and kindly friend.

Timothy opened his mouth to call him back, and shut it again as a bent old man came in sight. He wore a long green coat much faded by the weather, flapping limply round his calves. On his head was an old felt hat, doubtless gleaned from some gentleman's cast-off garments. It was tied on with a drab handkerchief, and from below its flapping brim his eyes stared fixedly before him, not watching the dip and dance of the bow as a normal player would do, concentrating merely on telling light from darkness. Brandy was on him almost before he had time to tuck the fiddle under his arm, and hold his stick defensively before him.

"Another step and I'll have your brains on the road."

Brandy halted, and as if in explanation gave an apologetic bark, wriggling closer until he stood right under the menacing stick.

"If it's not Seamus the fiddler!" breathed Timothy. "He was at the house not a week since and went off empty-handed—thanks to *her*. Of course he's almost stone-blind but if he hears anything—"

"How'd he know a dog's bark?" But without

being told Jane climbed softly over the low bank
and crouched down below road-level.

The old man laughed. "Ay, ay, I know you, my
fine fellow. You're a friendly one, and from a house
that—that—" He paused, sightless eyes screwed up
in thought. "I'm thinking that house isn't as friendly
as once it was, and if I'm right then you're far
from it. Just let's be certain sure." He fumbled
forward, tap-tap, tap-tap, and then the scrape
along the roadside began again. "Oh-h, here we
are." The stick had touched the milestone. He
bent, and as if he had eyes in the tips of his gnarled
fingers he felt the lichened numerals. "Ten from
Ballydoran and thirteen to Beleady. My boy, you're
a wheen of perches from home and I'm wondering
why."

The children waited, holding their breaths.
What if Brandy took a fancy to go with him, or
even tugged him towards them by the tails of his
coat?

The fiddler cupped his hands round his mouth and
halloo-ed: "WILL, WILL, WILL MAGUIRE!"

Brandy whined anxiously, beating his tail.

"Will Maguire, is it yourself? There's nary a head
of cattle nor sound of your curses, but where'd you
be but with your hound, and him so far from home?"

When only silence answered, he walked on slowly,
his shoulders drooping. Will was always good for a
meal or a ha'penny even if his new wife had other
notions of hospitality, and roads seemed longer and
friends fewer since—since— He began grumbling
to himself. "Times is changed. Ireland's not what
it was. No, nor me neither." Sighing, he flipped his

stick in the dog's direction. "Home with you, boy, you've nothing for me nor I for you."

Brandy heard dismissal in his tone, and pattered off to look for something more interesting.

As the fiddler passed the children his bony nose twitched and he tilted back his head, sniffed and "pointed" like a hound. For an instant Timothy wondered if he had really winded them but he trudged slowly on, and soon they heard his fiddle music once more. Slowly its notes thinned to an eerie sigh and slid out of earshot.

"In the country, everyone knows everyone and everyone's business," said Timothy, echoing his father. "That old fellow can see near as well as a sighted man. And then Bridie saying Barney Doggart had been this way too—that's two of them could be telling on us."

Jane nodded. Running away was not as easy as it had looked three days ago. They rose, and, more cautiously now, went down the road.

"Next time we hear anyone we'll just hide till they're away."

Jane sucked a scratched finger. "It'd be a deal easier if there weren't so many thorns and nettles and briars."

Timothy looked at her downcast face. "After the next milestone but one we'll stop and eat."

With this goal in view they stepped out well, and only saw one other wayfarer once in the two miles, when a man strolled past with a dozen roan-and-white bullocks. He was smoking a clay pipe and taking things easily while two quick-eyed dogs kept the herd in order.

It took both of them to control Brandy's excitement at the sight of his own kind, so they waited until the man had gone at least half a mile before they proceeded. Poor Brandy was quite unable to see rhyme and reason in their action. As they were now coming into a more thickly populated stretch of countryside, they decided to dodge cottages and farmhouses too. The two miles promised by Timothy stretched to at least double that before they went aside into a little clump of ash trees and sat down to eat and drink. It was very pleasant in the delicate green shade, and nightfall seemed far off, so by common consent they lingered, dabbling their feet in the stream that rilled by and licking the one bacon rib until it shone like ivory. "Some of Mama's things are ivory," boasted Timothy, rolling the bone between his palms to put a better sheen on it. "But I've a notion most of the bobbins are bone and that Uncle Alexander made them for her."

"She showed me them the once, when Granny wanted the lend of a thread. They—they"—she sought for the highest possible praise—"they could have belonged to any lady in the land, so they could."

Timothy said sheepishly, "I've them in the pack. You never thought I'd be leaving those behind me?" He began to unpack the bag. "We've hours before us. Let's just have a wee peep and I'll be telling you all she said before—before she went." He drew out the box and balanced it a moment in his hand. In spite of the sunshine he gave a little shiver. "She'd have wished it. Now that you're coming to Foyleside it's for the both of us."

He unwrapped the blue neckerchief and showed her the box and the poker-work lettering. She stroked the mother-of-pearl and felt the letters carefully as the blind man had felt the milestone. "Some day I'll be able to read every wee scrap of them." She wriggled with pleased anticipation. "Open it, do. What's holding you?"

He laid the trifles in a row on the neckerchief. "There's the letters of her name—" He pointed to the initials. "M. E.—Molly Erskine."

Jane laughed. "M—E. I know *that*. It's a real word. *Me*."

Oddly, it was the scrap of green brocade wrapped round the emery cloth which pleased her best. "If I were a grand lady I'd be having a gown of it. With a little short bodice and a long skirt with a frill that'd go rustle-rustle on the ground like the beech leaves I used to kick up when I was wee." She fingered the thread-holder as if its smoothness comforted her scratched hands.

Timothy dredged up an elusive memory. "That's all the way from India. It's ivory, and it was a sailor cousin of grandmother's brought it when he came back after going all round the world in a barque."

Jane put in, "My granny says that in the big house there was a—oh dear, the name's gone out of my head—something like harp it was, but anyway you played music on it for parties and balls, and the keys you played on were made of ivory."

They gazed in silence at the little worn objects, seeing in them all the world of travel and gentle-living and education which they had never known.

"And that?" asked Jane at last, laying a careful

finger on the linen at the very bottom of the box.

Timothy unfolded the tucker, with its lace edging worked with frail imaginary flowers. "It was hers, and her mother's before her."

"She'd be pretty in it." She folded it gently. "But she was always a pretty one."

"She was so." Without looking at her he re-packed the bag. A little wind fluttered the leaves above them and cast one down into the stream. It bobbed against a half-dozen pebbles and was gone round the next bend on its way to the big river, and thence perhaps to the lake which they must pass before they came into County Derry and Foyleside. "I wish we could run as fast as that. Still by now we'll likely be in the last corner of Donegal I showed you on the map. We'll see Fermanagh tomorrow."

"But where's Brandy? He's not been next nor nigh us since the drover came by."

They called from the shade of the trees, and then, since no one seemed to notice them, Timothy grew bolder and climbed a small hillock in the next field from which he had a view over several farms. Tentatively, he whistled. A few cows lowed in reply and rooks rose protesting from the haycocks, but no dog appeared.

They called and they whistled, they whistled and they called, but though other dogs answered, no eager bundle of tawny fur rushed gladly to meet them. They would even have been happy if he had come to give them a sulky nip, for after all he was a dog of spirit and they had practically throttled him when he followed his natural instincts in barking at his own kind.

"Best go back to the road. He'll find us there
when he's a notion to it." Timothy hitched up his
pack and led the way. They went on down the
road. The westering sun already was laying long
shadows in front of them, and presently they would
have to consider where they would spend the night.
The mislaying of Brandy—for surely it was no more
than that—weighed heavily on their spirits; they
walked in solemn single file in the grass at the edge
of the road.

They must have gone another mile and had
rounded a sharp corner when they heard a desolate
whine, and Brandy scrambled awkwardly over the
bank of the field. He stopped when he saw them,
ears and tail drooping, a front paw pathetically
raised.

Jane ran forward. "Oh Brandy, we thought you
were dead and gone. Are you much hurted?
Timothy—"

He was already kneeling before the dog. "He's
picked up a thorn, but Dear knows how I'll get it
out." Together they bent over the injured paw.
Brandy wagged his tail feebly and licked Jane's
ear. Timothy could see the thorn clearly enough
but his nails were so worn with constant outdoor
work that he could not grasp it, and feared to use
even the tip of his knife lest he do worse damage.
"The needle," breathed Jane. "What about the
needle in your Mama's wooden box?"

"You be holding him then." Timothy began to
search through his pack. They were so pre-occu-
pied that they never heard the swiftly approaching
carriage. The two greys drawing it were already

round the corner when they looked up and saw the
cruelly shod hooves almost upon them. Arms round
Brandy, heads down, they rolled against the grassy
bank and crouched there while the coachman swore
and tussled with his frightened beasts. The coach
rocked to a halt a few yards away, and an imperious
voice called, "What the devil's amiss, Thomas?
Have you taken leave of your senses?"

"It was the childer, my lord. I didn't see them
till I was on them. It's God's mercy we aren't all
dead in the ditch."

"You talk too much, Thomas." The owner of
the voice looked out of the window. He was a
florid, middle-aged gentleman with an exquisitely
folded cravat above a dove-coloured travelling
coat. He lifted a quizzing glass and surveyed the
children.

"The veriest tinker knows more than to squat on
the corner of a coach road."

Jane got to her feet and sketched a curtsey. "Sir,
if you please, our dog had picked up a thorn.
Please, my—my lord, don't be beating him."

The gentleman considered Brandy, and turned
to Timothy.

"H'm. He's the makings of a good game dog.
Mixed breed though ain't he, boy?"

"His dam was a pointer bitch, sir. Whisky they
called her, out of Lord Clanronald's estate, but—
there was a terrier running loose and—"

The gentleman gave what in the lower classes
would have been a knowing grin. "And so she
pupped. What do you call this fellow? Sherry?
Brandy?"

Timothy smiled back, forgetting that he was speaking to a lord. "Brandy, sir. My father has a notion to brandy—as a drink."

Another voice spoke from inside the carriage. "Let me see the children. The rest will do me good."

The gentleman put up his glass again. "They are tenant farmer's children, somewhat ragged. Speak to them if you will."

The lad perched behind the coach hastily dismounted and opened the door. The gentleman lifted his lady to the ground. Jane's eyes grew round, for the stuff of the lady's gown was daintier than the green brocade in Timothy's box. It was powder-blue with a pattern like rippled water on it and was caught at the base of her white neck with a dark blue jewel set in gold. The poke bonnet, the tiny kid shoes and the mittens matched the gown, the stole about her shoulders was surely swansdown, airy as a cloud, but her face was not so pretty as her clothes, for her eyes had dark shadows below them. Jane thought that she was foolish to travel along a bumpy road when she was so near to childbirth.

"Don't trouble yourself about them, Felicia," said her husband. "We might all be dead in a ditch by now, but—"

"But we are not, my lord." She looked Timothy up and down. "How old are you, boy?"

"Nearly twelve, my lady."

"And you?"

"Two months younger, my lady. We are cousins."

"Your mothers must have been pretty women, and meeting two fine sturdy children could be an omen." She spoke so softly that only Jane heard.

"Perhaps this time I will be fortunate too, and give my lord an heir." She beckoned to the lad. "Bring me the comfit box."

The boy came back with a small octagonal silver box. She held it out to Jane. Inside were small comfits, some rose-coloured, some purple, some pale yellow. "Take one. You too, boy."

They obeyed her. Jane took a purple one: it tasted just like the scented violets beside the beech wood. "Oh—h." Timothy chose a rose sweetmeat, his fingers feeling large as spades as he fumbled in the dainty box. "Thank you, my lady." It was strange as perfume in his mouth. The expression on his face made the gentleman laugh. "Yes boy, comfits are for the ladies. Well, shall we go on now, my lady? The horses will be chilled."

"Two more minutes. The air is so fresh." Her tired eyes lit on Brandy. "Did you say he had picked up a thorn? Thomas, see if you can ease the poor beast."

My lord muttered something which Timothy thought was the word "fidgets," but he could not be sure.

He shrugged. "Thomas, see to the dog." The lady watched the coachman's efforts for a minute, then said with gentle decision, "You are going the wrong way about it." She opened her reticule and drew out a small roll of white kid. "Take these tweezers. They are the exact instrument you need. Boy, hold the dog close."

Brandy stood like a rock, and when the painful little operation was over, sat down and licked his paw thoroughly.

The gentleman seemed much taken with this. "You might almost think he was a true-bred. What'd you take for him, boy?"

Jane's hand tightened on Timothy's. They looked mutely at the would-be purchaser for what felt a very long time before Timothy said: "I—my lord—we—we couldn't be selling him. He's a grand guard and we've a terrible long road to travel before we see my uncle's house on Foyleside."

"Please don't be taking him," said Jane. "We'd be heart-scared at nights but for him."

"You must not tease them, my lord. Dogs at least we have in plenty." The lady touched Jane's brown curls with her gloved hand. "He will not take your dog. But why are you alone?"

They explained lamely that no one wanted them in Sligo. "But my uncle has a fine farm on Foyleside, and no chick nor child of his own," said Timothy, hoping that this last bit was as true as it had been twelve years ago. "There'll be work for us and a welcome."

The lady crooked a finger at the lad. "Bring the other box from the door pocket."

As if by magic a larger silver box was opened before them. "My pastry cook's famous macaroons," said the lady. As the children approached warily she said in romantic tone, "You are as shy as a pair of pigeons from my dovecot." Her husband sniffed.

They accepted the crisp nutty little cakes. The flavour was delicious, quite unlike anything they had ever tasted. The lady laughed, and Timothy suddenly felt he was being treated as if he were her lap dog, and not like himself at all. Jane only wondered how soon the child would be born and if it would be as pretty and delicate as its mother.

Timothy said: "If you please sir, we must be on our way. And the near grey's shivering."

"So she is. You've eyes under that rough thatch." He steered his wife towards the carriage. As her foot was on the step she said something to him. He called to Thomas: "Take the brats and their dog up with you, and go easy."

The children did as they were bid. They crouched and clung on, certain that the next rut on the road would jerk them off. The miles flashed by, a village was left behind and beyond it they drove between well-tilled fields. Timothy had just seen another milestone when the carriage drew to a halt.

"My lord, if the childer are for Foyleside and we for Lord Dunlinn's, I must be setting them down. They've had all of eight miles."

"Just so."

They climbed down stiffly, and while Brandy yawned, came and made their thanks. Jane dipped an extra curtsey. "My lady, I'll be thinking of you and wishing you well."

The lady smiled and selected a sixpence from her reticule. "Now my pretty, if you go to the farmhouse by the next road-ends, and say that Lady Felicia sent you, you will be given sup and let sleep under cover."

"Felicia—" said his lordship despairingly. "We are late already—"

Thomas took the hint. With a wink at Timothy he clicked his tongue at the horses, adding, as they moved off, "Anyways we've got you safe into

Fermanagh. But no more spraughling across the road or you'll never see Foyleside."

A gloved hand waved from the window. The carriage turned off the main road towards a great house set among woodland.

The children were left alone. Now that the harness no longer rattled they could hear birds chirping and the sound of a river, flowing swiftly towards the lake marked on Timothy's map.

"Fermanagh," said Timothy. "Oh now we're well on the way. We've nothing to do but follow the lakeside till we see Enniskillen."

Chapter Five

JOHN CAPPLE'S CAVE

THEY WALKED ON, Brandy treading carefully at their heels, and in a very short time saw a big white farmhouse. It looked most prosperous. Nearby was a strip planted with greenstuff Jane had never seen before, turnip, and a few acres of oats, the first they had set eyes on since they left home. Timothy thought another green crop which Jane could not name must be flax, and broke a tough stem to show her the white fibre inside it. "They'll be far too grand to trouble themselves with us."

"Lady Felicia said—" They argued it up and down, pride fighting a losing battle with visions of a bright fire and well-spread supper table. Dew was rising now and Timothy felt his thin shirt cold on his back. He shivered and Jane said almost tearfully, "I've no greater notion to begging than you have, but Lady Felicia—" She pulled him on by the hand and they went up to the back door of the house. It stood wide open and within they saw a stout woman bustling round, now stirring the pot over the fire, now turning the oatcake on the harnen stand, now settling a great pitcher of milk on the table. They watched her, fascinated, not daring to speak until she turned to pick up a pail near the door and saw them. "If it's not tinker brats again. I've had a bellyful of them today. Get along with you and wheedle another body for a change."

They nudged each other, scarlet with shame. "Lady Felicia—" croaked Timothy. "She—she was sending us to—to ask for a night's lodging."

The woman rolled up her eyes. "Her ladyship. Dear help us, she's as many hangers-on as I've boiling fowl. Since my sister was her wet-nurse, she thinks she owns the whole family." She considered them. "Now, you'll get your supper and you can lie in the hay, and when milking time comes you'll do your share. That content you?"

Jane, head downbent, muttered a thank-you.

"At least the cat's not got your tongue."

"We—could—I have—" Timothy drew out the pence Bridie had refused.

She almost struck them from his hand. "As if I'd take a beggar's ha'pence! What are you doing alone anyways? What's happened to your parents?" As she spoke she was clapping porridge into bowls. She poured a liberal stream of buttermilk and handed the foodstuff to them. "When you've scraped those clean, you can make yourselves scarce before himself comes along. And if you're wanting to get on the right side of him, see the dog's tied up."

Brandy looked at her. T't-t'ting between her teeth she scooped up more porridge and plumped it into a hollow in the yard. "Great dogs to feed too! Ay, it's easy for the likes of her ladyship to be preaching at other folk."

Brandy was not proud. He licked the stones clean and they all went quietly into the hayshed. The carriage and the sweetmeats and the macaroons were dreamlike and distant, all the excitement of them taken out by a stout housewife who made excellent porridge and whose buttermilk was far better than Grandmother's ever had been. They stayed in the shed without speaking, feeling ashamed and sad and angry as they had never done with Bridie. However, the hay was comfortable and the day had been long. Timothy began to feel warm again. Jane and Brandy curled down together. They slept before the farmer came in late from haying and never saw him stand at the door and look down on them, and then gently put an extra lock of hay over Jane's bare feet.

Some time in the dawn Timothy woke himself

up by sneezing and could not sleep again. He lay wondering in a muddled way whether they should slip off before milking time, or wait in the hopes of breakfast. He did not feel hungry, but his throat was hot and dry, and he longed for the spring water he had left behind him on his father's farm. Taking a drink from the pump by the kitchen door would wake everyone and bring down wrath upon their heads: he must wait.

Perhaps he dozed, for the next he knew was a rough hand shaking his shoulder. "Stir your stumps, lad—and your sister as well. The beasts are waiting."

Indeed they were, but the children were strangers to them and they to the children, so they did not let down their milk readily. The mistress of the house surveyed their scant pailfuls grimly. "You'll never make your fortunes by milking. Well for My Lady Castlepitchfork to be telling me what to do. Och don't stand there gaping. Come away in and you'll get what's waiting for you."

It was more porridge. They swallowed it down, and as bidden placed their rinsed bowls on the dresser. Just then the master of the house came in. He glanced over at them. "Good luck on the road," he said and sat down to his own meal. As they turned to go he winked at them.

They went back to the coach road. When they topped the slight rise they saw a long blade of silver water, shimmering in the early sunlight: the lake whose course they must follow. Half a mile further on a gig drew to a halt beside them. The farmer whom they had seen at breakfast leant out.

"I'd as lief have company as not." He grinned at their astonishment. "Sure, her bite's worse nor her bark, and a still tongue's the only answer. In with you. I've a cow with a torn udder, and the apothecary at Beleady might have a salve to suit her."

He was a pleasant as his wife had been cross. He took them clear through Beleady and set them down on the lake road. "Now your way's clear to Enniskillen, and there's a wheen of haystacks for you to sleep under, and caves in the hillside, come to that, though you'd do best to keep clear of John Capple's cave."

"John Capple?" asked Jane. "The highwayman? John the Horse, my granny calls him."

"That's the fellow. He rides as if the Devil himself were in his heels. Once, when a horse went lame under him, and he had to dismount, he hamstrung the beast so that no one else could ride it."

The children looked at him, aghast. This was a tale they had not heard, and each secretly vowed never to seek shelter in a cave used by such a character.

The farmer grinned at their expressions and gave them a double handful of ripe yellow gooseberries and a thickly buttered farl. "I'll never miss it. I carry overmuch weight already." He flicked the horse and was off before they could thank him.

His kindness eased Jane's doldrums, though Timothy's head felt thick and his legs heavy. If it had not been for Jane he might have lain down in the nearest shelter and slept the clock round. He was thirsty too, and wondered idly if the spring at

Foyleside would be as refreshing as the one on his father's farm, and that led him on to a thought he had never admitted before: was the long journey, the lack of food, the poor lodging worth the trouble? Or were they looking for the end of the rainbow?

Yet the way was pleasant. The lake was scattered with small wooded islands standing on their own wavering reflections. The water whispered among the reeds and the sun shone gently through a high veil of cloud. They did not see anyone who knew them, only local farmers going about their work, and these passed with the merest nod.

When they stopped, on Jane's request, to eat the remainder of Bridie's bacon and the soda farl and the gooseberries, Timothy would take only the fruit. "My mouth's dry. Anything else would choke me."

"Yesterday there was no filling you. What's amiss?" She looked intently at him, then laid her warm hand on his forehead. "Why! You're hot as fire! You'll have caught a chill with the wetting we had before the night at Bridie's."

He shrugged off her solicitude and strode off at a great rate. Ugh, how anyone could eat cold bacon— He ran into a side loaning and was sick before she caught up with him.

She eyed him doubtfully.

"If you look like that I'll be sorry I ever brought you," he threatened.

"You didn't bring me. I came. And if I hadn't, where'd you be now? Lying at the bottom of a ditch after the tinkers had cut your throat."

They glared at each other, like rival cats watching for the first sign of weakness. Presently Jane walked on, head high, feeling hurt and frightened: she never fought with Timothy. Never. She tried not to look back at him and just as the temptation was almost irresistible, she was saved by a great hullaballoo behind them—running feet and a woman's voice raised in exasperated mirth. "It's the Devil himself got into your skins. Stop, or I'll tan the spots off you."

Both of them whirled about, fearing that their hostess of last night had found them out in some crime. Instead they only saw a stout oldish woman waddling down the road in a vain chase of three black-and-pink piglets.

"Stop them or they'll run all the fat off. Turn them at the loaning—quick, there's long enough legs on you and not a breath left in my body—"

Through all her grumbling her long mouth still smiled as if at a secret joke. Jane had never seen anyone smile and scold at the same time, and watched fascinated.

"Get on, get on daughter! You'll see me driven astray in the head if you're not giving a hand this instant minute."

They had helped a hundred times in just such a situation. Jane flung herself at one pig, Brandy at another, Timothy belatedly at the third. Jane staggered back against the bank clasping her grunting catch, Brandy halted his in mid-career, and teeth bared, hackles raised, dared it to go further until the woman panted up, slapped it soundly on the rump as she would have slapped a

wilful child, and seized hold of the curly tail.
"Now my fine fellow, mind your manners or you'll
never make old bones."

Still clasping her pig, Jane giggled. Who ever
heard of a pig making old *bones*—bacon, yes. She
shook with laughing, even when the woman took
her charge from her.

Timothy had not been so clever. His pig had
dodged into the rushes, and now was sinking to its
belly, squealing for help.

The woman let her stick drop. "Here, girl dear,
give him a hold of that and pull like the Devil or
they'll both be drownded." She began to urge her
two pigs down the loaning, while between them the
children extracted the third pig. "That's the way of
it," she called. "Now he'll be off for the midden like
a bird."

Jane began to laugh again. Timothy sluiced off
the worst of the mud and said nothing. The woman
had guessed correctly, once in the lane the pigs
dashed down to the untidy farmyard at the foot of
it— "They'll do rightly now." She dug in her
pocket and brought out a poke of blue paper.
"They're all I've on me. Mint lozengers, powerful
good for the stomach." She cocked her head at
Timothy. "You look kind of peaky. They'll put
heart into you."

Indeed, the sharp taste was refreshing. Even
Timothy gave her a half-smile. "You'll be for
Enniskillen," she hazarded. "You've the look of
travelling people. Like my son Johnny—" She broke
off. "Dear help me, if they're not round by the
back of the house already." Away she trotted,

shouting over her shoulder: "Mind now, if you're this way again you'll be welcome." She was at the midden by now. "You wild ones you!"

The children walked on slowly chewing their mints. Jane was still inclined to giggle, Timothy was muddy and miserable. He did not wave at the stage coach as it rolled past, and when they met a soldier in scarlet uniform with blue facings, he did not even glance sideways at him, though Jane beamed her admiration. At that she forgot the funny pigs and their owner and began to worry. Timothy must be really ill. Nothing else would account for his glum behaviour. Somehow, though she had imagined perils of bogs and storms and footpads and tinkers and drunken men, she had never thought that either of them could be ill. Why on earth had she let herself be overcome by his tales of Foyleside? All the same, thoughts of the quiet white house with the glowing fire and its herd of cows and its boat and its kindly owner were beguiling. If only, as in the old tales, they could put on the wings of the magical fairy people, and jump over the remaining miles. But they couldn't, and to turn back now would invite endless punishment: indeed, probably both of them would be flung out to fend for themselves. She sighed, and felt round her mouth for the very last traces of that heartening mint.

The road narrowed here, clasped between the rushy verge of the water and the steeply rising bluffs of the Fermanagh Hills. There was no room for farms on this narrow shore, and the only sign of habitation was a tiny shack by the lakeside beside which a boat was moored. The clouds had covered the sun by now, and the air puffed moistly in their faces, promising drizzle.

Timothy took off the plaid he had wrapped from shoulder to waist and drew it tightly round him as if it were a December afternoon. Jane could almost hear her grandmother saying: "Get that boy into the warm afore he drops." But apart from the fisherman's hut there were neither houses nor hay-stacks in the neighbourhood. As if he caught the echo of her thoughts Timothy pointed to a darker shadow on the bluff just ahead of them. "By the thorn bush—would it be a cave? Maybe we could wait there a wee while."

When they reached the thorn bush they found behind it a cave with a double entrance, divided by a pillar of rough limestone. From its mouth a stream bubbled over mossy boulders, and was channelled under the road into the lake, but above the level of the stream was a dry rocky shelf. They followed it a few yards so as to get out of the wind, and then when it turned a corner came into dark-ness. Jane thought of the farmer's remark that morning about caves. "I—I wonder—" she began. Her voice rang hollow, and she looked up, startled, to see that the narrow entrance had led into a wide cavern whose ceiling she could barely discern, though as her eyes grew accustomed to the dimness she saw what looked like great stone icicles dangling from the roof. Immediately below them, across the stream, tapering stone pillars gleamed moistly as they were fed by the limestone water dripping from the roof. The many drops played a hollow irregular tune, like that of a disordered clock, curiously disturbing, quite unlike the gentle babble of the stream.

Jane said with a cheerfulness she did not feel, "We'll be nicely away from the rain here."

Timothy nodded like a sleep-walker. His throat was dry as a kiln. His ears were ringing. All he wanted was to lie down and be left in peace. "It's very cold," he muttered.

With all her heart Jane longed for a dry haystack into which he could sink and sweat off the fever, but the nearest shelter was the fisherman's hut. There might be dry rushes there, and it would be better for her to go and bring some back than to drag him out into the gathering rain.

"Promise you'll stay here with Brandy, and I'll have dry bedding for you before you've time to turn over."

He nodded, and sank down to the ground, as if his knees had given under him, head against the cool damp stone. "Don't be long." His eyes searched her anxiously before they closed. "Sorry . . ." She took off her shawl and tucked it under him, then tried to push Brandy against him for extra warmth. Obediently the dog settled down, his warm bulk glowing over Timothy's cold legs.

Jane hesitated, wishing that she could be in two places at once. She must go and yet—and yet, suppose he wandered off while she was away and she lost him in the caves and they never reached Foyleside, and—

Before she could terrify herself any more she ran from the cave into the fast-paling light. Even in the midst of her anxiety it was a relief to be out of that gloomy place, but as she bent her head against the drizzle she could not help wishing pettishly that County Fermanagh were a hot sunny place like the far country where that ivory had come from. She reached the fisherman's hut more quickly than she had expected. They must have been walking at a crawl that afternoon. It looked just the same, except that now the boat was missing: doubtless its owner had gone on a fishing trip before the light failed. She approached carefully, her bare feet noiseless among the rushes and tangle of driftwood.

A coot clucked nearby in the reeds. Rain pattered on the water. Nothing else stirred, not an oar, not a fishing rod. Even the road was deserted. She peered into the open side of the shelter. At the back of it lay kindling and a heap of dry rushes. She lifted these to reveal a tinder box and a soft bundle done up in a red handkerchief. She longed for the tinder box but dared not touch it, for even if they used it, smoke and fire would excite too much notice. The handkerchief was different. She untied the knot and not so much forgot as pushed out of sight all Grandmother's teaching about honesty, for there lay a thick packet of potato farls, inter-leaved with lean bacon. Her mouth watered. What good would it do Timothy if she and Brandy went hungry? She took the bottom two farls and ate a slice of bacon and half a piece of potato bread; the other slice and a half would do for Brandy.

She retied the handkerchief and covered it again. If she took an armful of rushes for Timothy, puffed up the remainder and then lay gently on them to give them a used look—

A duck squattered down into the water and as the ripples calmed down she heard the regular clack and swish of oars. She snatched up the rushes and fled up the bank and along the road as if every horseman in Fermanagh were on her heels. If she had tried to look guilty she could not have acted better. Luckily, there was nothing to see her except startled water-fowl, and on this wet evening the wild-fowlers had stayed at home and did not hear them.

She did not stop until she reached the cave. Her hair was drenched with fine rain and her gown clung damply about her, but fright made her warm as a trotting pony.

She hurried over to Timothy. The light was much dimmer now and she had to pick her steps carefully, but she could see he was not where she had left him, but was now sprawled face down, Brandy still across his legs. The cuffs of his shirt were wet as if he had been dabbling in the stream, though he did not reply when she questioned him. The dog rose, whining anxiously, and Jane was so pleased to have something warm and friendly near her that she kissed the top of his russet head before spreading the dry reeds as a bed for his master. It took a great deal of pushing and pulling to persuade Timothy to lie down on them and allow her to tuck both shawl and plaid securely round him. He mumbled that he was thirsty, so she filled his noggin with water from the stream and put it to his lips. He drank and pushed it aside irritably. His hands were fiery to the touch, and shaking as if he were out in a snow-storm. Jane told herself that once he had slept on a warm bed he would soon throw off the chill and be

well again. Why only last winter she herself—
She shuddered over the memory of Granny's possets
and purges, but next morning she had been fresh as
new milk. She wished she had those medicines now
for Timothy, but he was a boy and much stronger
than she, so doubtless he would recover all the
more quickly.

However, as the night wore on and the damp
struck through her thin gown, she could not pre-
tend even to herself to be cheerful. No one could
have chosen a worse place in which to have a fever.
Even Brandy's pelt was chill to the touch. The
water's hollow voice nagged at her, like a scolding
which never ends. Every sigh, every movement,
every drip from the roof echoed, and the long unex-
plored recesses behind them distorted the little
sounds and sent back new and unrecognizable
voices. She could not keep those winding caverns
out of her mind. No matter how she tried, her fears
asked endless questions. How far under the mountain did they run? Did anyone—or anything—live
in them? Rats and bats and farm cats run wild,
mad dogs or—or even bears or lions escaped from
some fair. But that was silly. She gave a watery
smile over those fancies. The place was much more
likely to be inhabited by poor wanderers like themselves—or by highwaymen looking for a place to
hide their booty. She remembered the farmer's
warning. Was this indeed John Capple's cave, and
might he not return at any moment? Or suppose
the stream rose in sudden spate, and drowned them
as Granny drowned unwanted kittens. Granny had
a tale too of a huge blind fish washed out of a cave

on Lough Gill shore after a winter storm: it was
dead and limp—she said—as a gutted herring, but
her grandfather's father had seen its ghost. In this
cave too there could be ghosts. She remembered a
tag of Granny's in the old tongue: the *Sidhe*—the
fairy people. Where could they live but here?

She sprang to her feet and stumbled to the mouth
of the cave. She leaned there, shaking, taking deep
breaths of the free, unenclosed air, that smelled of
grass instead of damp rock and water-washed
stones. The rain had passed and moonlight gleamed
on the road and the rushes and the peaceful lough.
A coot was still talking to itself, and she forgot that
she had been brought up, as Granny said, "like a
heathen" and prayed that the saint who looked
after waterfowl would bless it. She shut her eyes
and soaked in the peace, and when Brandy came up
and rubbed against her legs, she jumped as if he had
bitten her. It took all her resolution to go back to
Timothy. He stirred on the rushes as she bent
over him and clutched at her with those terrify-
ingly hot shaking hands, mouthing something
she could hardly catch, thought it might have
been ". . . Foyleside . . ."

"We'll start again tomorrow, truly we will. But
just talk to me a minute—oh please, please
Timothy."

Brandy pressed against her, puzzled by her tone,
doing his best to understand.

It was no use. Quite apart from John Capple,
the glimpse of the outside world had made the
cave even more terrifying. The walls seemed to
press in upon her, carrying with them echoes of

air and water, voices and half-words. She no longer realized the difference between imaginary sounds and those she really heard, she only knew that if Timothy and she stayed any longer, he would never get better. It was a bad place, like the country round Bridie's cottage.

She shut her eyes and put her hands over her ears. How long ago this afternoon seemed with its funny silly pigs and a mock-angry pig-woman. She let her hands fall. That was it. "If you're this way again, you'll be welcome." They must go to her house.

She bent and hugged Brandy. "Sit, Brandy, sit." Reluctantly the dog sank down across Timothy's legs, and, sighing, closed his eyes.

When she had made sure Timothy was well covered she said clearly in his ear: "I'll not be long and then we'll be off to Foyleside. Wait here for me."

The moonlight was stronger now and she was able to run out of the cave and on down the road without bruising her bare toes. It was pure bliss to be in the open and on a plain solid road.

When she arrived at the cottage it slept peacefully in the moonlight, and only a grunt or two from the pigsty disturbed the quiet.

The memory of Timothy and Brandy in the cave forced her to disturb the peace. After three attempts she rapped on the door. The sole answer was a cheerful snoring. That made her angry. How dare anyone sleep when poor Timothy was shivering in the horrible cave. She knocked until she bruised her knuckles. "It's only the girl who helped you with the wee pigs."

"What d'you say—" The voice was slurred with sleep. There was a sound of something hard and heavy bumping on the floor. "You ruffians you, waking an honest woman at this hour. Away with you, or you'll be running off with sore heads and bloody noses."

"It's only me—the girl who helped with the pigs."

"*Me*, she says, *me*. Who's *me*—the cat's cousin?"

The latch on the top half of the door was lifted and the pig-woman peered out, a stout blackthorn stick in one hand. When she saw Jane she lowered it and shook her head.

"And what is a decent wee girl like yourself doing out at this hour?"

Jane began to explain.

"The cave—!" burst in the woman. Her whole face changed. Her eyes rolled in her head as if she were going to have a fit. "Are you clean crazed? Thon's where—where—where all manner of rogues and footpads hide when they're on the run. Everyone knows that—" Her voice rose to a wild scream. "And who knows it better than I do." She snatched up a shawl and tucked it tightly about her. "I could have telled you thon boy had a fever on him. Not a haet of sense between the pair of you." She laid more turfs on the fire, swung the pot lower above it, took a homespun blanket off the box bed and tossed it to Jane. It reeked of turf smoke but was warm—and odorous—as a fleece. "Hold you that, child. He'll be needing it. If I yoked the ass into the cart—"

The cart was a low rickety platform on wheels,

with side pieces across which a plank was laid to serve as a seat. Despite her bulk, the pig woman soon had the drowsy donkey backed between the shafts. She made Jane lead him while she stayed in the cart. "And stop calling me 'you'. I'm Mrs Ann Molony these forty years past." She settled her ample self, tucked the blackthorn stick under her arm, and they started.

One thing Jane longed to know, but she never had half a chance to ask the question, for Mrs Molony talked cheerfully without pause, giving her an account of almost every object within miles of her cottage—except one: the cave.

At last Jane got the question out. "The—highwayman, him they call John Capple. Would he be in the cave?"

"You wouldn't be walking here, if he was. He was heading for Derry last I heard tell of him—a month since. What he's hid in the cave is his own business, and the sooner we're all out of it the better I'll be pleased. Don't speak of it to anyone, or you'll have me to deal with as well as John Capple himself."

Jane quavered, "Wh-what would he be leaving there?"

Mrs Molony's grimace melted into a strained smile. She said in flat reasonable tones which made the words all the more terrifying, "He's on the run for killing one man and robbing another. Where the stuff he got may be, or where the bones of the other fellow—John's the only one knows that. Keep his name off your tongue. It's not lucky."

"I—I heard—when I was in the cave—I heard—"

Mrs Molony's bright little eyes looked suddenly as hard as steel. She bent towards Jane and growled, "Hold your whisht, unless you're wanting me to turn round and leave you to it."

Her look frightened Jane as much as her words. Of her own accord she clapped the donkey on the rump and dragged him forward. "Hurry!"

"He's only the one pace, and we'll have to thole it."

To Jane they seemed to be going no faster than a snail, but at last they reached the cave. For a long minute Mrs Molony waited before it, then dropped to her knees and crossed herself with solemn deliberation.

It was too much for Jane. With a cry of "Timothy! Brandy! Timothy!" she ran in.

The cave was almost as she had left it. Timothy had slipped sideways from his rushy mattress, but Brandy still lay beside him, and when she drew breath, all the noises of water, the scent of wet rocks and earth, and the feeling of pressure and unseen presences were potent as ever. Indeed, she was even more frightened, having heard for a second time that it was a robber's haunt, and knowing that John Capple had had plenty of time to return here from Derry. Why, he might be only half a mile away down the road. He might be watching Mrs Molony and the donkey at this moment. Come to that, even Mrs Molony frightened her. With shaking hands she pulled Timothy upright, and, supporting him against her shoulder, staggered towards the entrance. He did his best to help, but his limbs worked like those of a doll stuffed with sawdust. They would have sprawled together at the entrance had not Mrs Molony come to meet them. Still muttering prayers under her breath she got both arms about the boy and hauled him out into the moonlight. "This place would put my heart cross-wise." She glanced back, sweat gleaming on her forehead. "Dear help us, what's that?" From deep within the cave came a long sighing sound. There was a slow rumble, a splash, a rush of water, and then silence closed over once more.

The three of them, with Brandy circling anxiously about them, made for the cart. Somehow Timothy was hoisted on to it, and they started back at what was as near a gallop as the donkey could compass. Mrs Molony drove, Jane ran alongside, trying to hold Timothy on the cart, and Brandy cavorted gaily through the rushes. Breathless, they reached the cottage, and still panting, set to work. Timothy was propelled on to Mrs Molony's bed. Jane was told to strip him and rub him down with a cloth dipped in a bucket of warm water, while Mrs Molony heated buttermilk and forced it down his throat. Lastly, the cloth with which he had just been washed was wrung out in well-water and laid on his head. Jane also hung his clothes up to dry, unharnessed the donkey, prepared the truckle bed and brought in armfuls of hay. At last she was told to lie down and sleep on the sweet-smelling grasses. "Don't be fretting, daughter. He'll be lively as a trout by next nightfall."

Mrs Molony bolted the door. Brandy lay down beside Jane. Timothy muttered something—did he say "money" or was it "morning"?—and seemed to sleep. Jane's last memory, before her own eyes closed, was of Mrs Molony fingering her rosary and thanking the saints for safe delivery; she said other things too, but Jane could not make out the muddled words.

When they awoke, sunlight was already lighting up the bed where Timothy slept. As Jane stirred, Brandy opened one eye. Above the turf fire the black pot steamed lazily.

Jane felt a great load slip off her shoulders. John Capple had no place here. Everything was going to be all right. Already they had come almost half way, and soon they would be back on the road to Foyleside once more.

Chapter Six

JOHNNY'S MOTHER

S HE WAS SO happy and so secure that she drifted
off to sleep again, but was soon roused and set
to work. She had to do all the tasks she had once
done for Granny, with the difference that while
Granny nagged at her all the time Mrs Molony
only gave a laugh, or at most an almost affectionate
cuff, when Jane made a mistake. Nothing seemed
to wipe off her smile for long. She talked all the

time, and sometimes what she said did not make sound sense, but after that night in the cave any human voice sounded delightful.

For a few hours Timothy lay quietly in bed, dozing and waking, quite incurious as to how he had come here, seemingly forgetful of the night's doings. Long before nightfall, however, he had coaxed Brandy over to sit near him. When Mrs Molony touched his forehead she found it quite cool. "You'll be hungry soon," she pronounced, "but tonight you'll make do on gruel and buttermilk. Tomorrow will tell a different tale."

Timothy protested, but when he rose his legs bent like rush stems. Mrs Molony laughed at him, as she laughed at so many things. "Sleep it away son, you'll be running like a redshank in less than no time."

She was quite right. By the afternoon of the next day Timothy could have eaten the whole batch of potato farls which she baked.

"What'd I tell you?" said Mrs Molony to Jane. She smoothed a tress of hair away from Jane's eyes. "It's like having my own back. But they're all scattered. Bridget's in service in Sligo and her wee sister's married on a Donegal man and has an apronful of her own childer. Seamus and Patrick went to Americky. And Johnny—Johnny—" All the laughter fell out of her face, her mouth went square as if it uttered a soundless scream, her eyes were wild as those of a cornered beast. "Johnny." The word seemed like a gag in her mouth. She turned away. Jane pretended to be putting fresh turfs on the fire. When she looked up again

Mrs Molony's eyes were twinkling just as usual.
"While Johnny remembers me, so I live comfortable
enough, but the nights do be so long, and without
childer the place is empty as a drawn well. But
you're here now." Her smile embraced Jane and
reached out to include Timothy and Brandy.

Jane did not often kiss even her grandmother,
but now she kissed Mrs Molony: it was so terrible
to grow old and live alone. Afterwards, when
Timothy had yawned himself to sleep (on the
truckle bed tonight), she whispered, "He doesn't
remember the cave at all."

"All the better." She emphasized her words
with finger-taps on Jane's knee. "You be forgetting
it too, and John Capple. He's no good to you—nor
to himself neither." She looked beyond Jane into
the fire's heart. As if she saw a picture there and
were describing it she said very slowly, "Soon that
one will die alone on the roadside like the mad dog
he is. And there'll be only one to send up a prayer
for him. Soon." The word rustled in the room.
Brandy started awake, his hair rising on his neck.
Then a turf collapsed sideways and Mrs Molony
rose stiffly, as if she were older than Jane's grandmother and shot the bolts on the door. She stood
staring at it, as if it might spring to attack her,
lost in a world Jane could not enter, and then it
was as if a different woman spoke. "Now I'll heat
us a drop of milk and then we'll be off to our beds."

Next day was so clear and bright that the
children would have liked to start for Enniskillen,
but Mrs Molony insisted that Timothy was not
yet fit for the road.

The day after that Timothy was blunter. "We'll have to be on our way. We're eating you out of house and home."

Her ready laugh rang out. "What's a side of bacon for but eating? Sure I'm having the time of my life, it's as if Mary and Johnny and Thomas were back and licking their bowls clean."

She wheedled them on from day to day, giving Timothy titbits to strengthen him, telling Jane endless, and pointless, tales about Terence and Kate and Thomas and Johnny—always she came back to Johnny. When Timothy tackled her again, days later, she had another excuse handy. "You'd never want to miss Beleady fair, would you? I've a pig ready to go, so the pair of you could be helping me."

"But it's the wrong direction—it's Enniskillen we're making for."

"Now son, you'd not deny me the pleasure of putting a bit of flesh on your ribs—you could rattle a stick over them." She roared with laughter over her own jest.

The next four days were going to be a waste of time, but she had been kind, and they had no wish to hurt her. However, it was odd that despite the good food and the comfortable bed Timothy longed for a night in the open, where they would be free. Mrs Molony—he shook his head as if he were shaking off a cobweb. She was so kind, so jolly most of the time, but there were things about her he could not understand. Only yesterday he had overheard her talking nonsense to the pigs, and then, when one nuzzled roughly at the pail she carried, she picked up a stick and belaboured the creature unmercifully. Then just as suddenly she dropped the stick, seemed to forget it and came back to the house. He said nothing of this to Jane, merely wished that fair-day was over.

On fair-day Mrs Molony jogged off in the ass cart, the pig securely tied, the children and Brandy walking behind. They caught up with others making for Beleady, and Mrs Molony hailed them all, though none of them came to walk alongside. Still, they arrived safely, and the children saw with thankfulness that they need not fear recognition here. They were each given a penny and left to their own devices.

If only Timothy had brought his pack and plaid with them it would have been an excellent chance to escape, but it seemed silly to miss the evening meal, or even be overtaken on the way by Mrs Molony. One more night would make no difference. So they wandered off.

It was a very modest fair. On either side of the wide sloping street stood rickety stalls. A few women presided over baskets of farm produce, a boy squatted dispiritedly by a bunch of hill sheep, and Mrs Molony's pig was the fattest of a lean dozen.

Jane bought a ribbon with her penny. "So's I'll look tidy when we get to Foyleside." She held it up for Timothy to see, its delicate blue making her weather-stained gown seem even drabber. But it gave him an idea. "We'd never be able to repay her for all the stuff we've eaten, but we could buy her one or two wee things." Jane nodded. She drew

Timothy into a corner, pulled out the little linen bag which held all her money, and gave him a shilling.

"Lady Felicia gave me sixpence of it, and if Mrs Molony hadn't taken you in when you'd the fever—"

"What'll we get, then? Wait till I've my sixpence out." He groped in his pocket, and a puzzled look came over his face. "I—I thought I'd it all tied up in a wee flat bag, but some must have come loose." He withdrew his hand. In it lay the little bag, two coins, such as he had never owned in his whole life—a round thick five-shilling bit and a guinea piece, bright as the day it was minted —and a thin water-worn pebble.

Just as Jane reached forward Mrs Molony came up. Timothy let his hand fall to his side, but gold shines brightly on a sunny day in a lackpenny village, and they could not be sure whether or not she had seen it. Certainly she looked them over more carefully than usual, and this time her ready smile was awry. "What's the two of you plotting?"

Timothy put a bold face on it. "Sure, Jane's spent her penny on a bit of ribbon! I'm getting more for my money."

The wary look dropped from her face. She gave him a hearty buffet across the shoulders. "Mind you do, boy. But don't be roaming off." She trotted away.

Jane turned back to Timothy. "Where did you find the money? Oh Timothy, you—you wouldn't be stealing it?" And in real alarm: "You're not ill again?"

Indeed he had turned pale as a tallow candle. He shook his head. "No. Not ill. But I've remembered. The cave's been like a dream, all noises and things I wasn't sure of, and feeling cold and hot and thirsty. I knew you'd told me to lie quiet, but I couldn't bear the sound of the water so near when my mouth was like a kiln. And then I crawled over to take a sup of water—"

"But you shouldn't have. You might have drowned."

"Well, I didn't, though my head was spinning. I took a wee sup and then I'd a notion that sucking a pebble would take the heat out of my mouth." He held up his clenched hand, unfolded it, and shut it quickly again. "In amongst the pebbles were the coins. When I saw them I sang out to Brandy, 'We're rich, boy.' But by then the cave was going this way and that and I couldn't tell if the noises were in my head or out of it. I jammed my hand into my pocket—"

"That's why your sleeve was wet."

"None of it was real at all. I was sick as a dog and heart-scared. Next thing was waking up to see you and Mrs Molony in the morning light. The fever and the wet and cold and the noises were all gone and I didn't want to think of them. I didn't even feel in the pocket."

Jane was pale as he. "John Capple—John the Horse. The man the farmer told us hamstrung a horse that had gone lame under him, so's to spoil the creature for anyone else. The farmer said he could be in the cave—and Mrs Molony dropped a hint—"

"John Capple. *J.C.* On the bit of my map that shows the road to Enniskillen it says *J.C.'s cave.* He'll have dropped the money. There could be more away at the back in a dark crack."

Jane seized his arm. "Don't be going back again. Not for all the gold in the world. I'll away home and leave you if you do."

"You needn't trouble yourself, I've no heart for it."

"Then let's go. Mrs Molony——"

"I'll be buying something for her first. I'd never look my uncle in the face if I was so tight-fisted. It's the least we can do."

Head downbent, Jane nodded. But the sunshine had gone out of the day. With her in silent attendance Timothy made a round of the stalls and bought a piece of honeycomb. This was laid on two large cabbage leaves, another leaf put over it and the whole fragile parcel bound lightly by a twist of hay. "Hold it level, boy, or it'll all run away afore you reach home." He paid over the twopence demanded and screwed up his eyes over a laboriously inscribed label: *Tee, STRAIGHT from The Indies. Sixpence to buy What Will Maik 2 Strong POTT-FULLS.* He bought the twist of paper containing the precious stuff.

Jane sighed blissfully as she took the cabbage leaves from him. "Lady Felicia would sup tea maybe twice a day. Look, there's a new stall round that corner."

They went over to find an old man putting out cups and plates and dishes: some decorated with pictures of fish, some quite plain, and a few delicate.

trifles of creamy porcelain whose inner surface shone like petals of a pale yellow pansy. "Oh-h." Jane bent over them. "Granny's told me how pretty Beleady china is many and many's a time."

"Then your Granny's telled you no word of a lie." The dealer summed them up: their poor clothes, their eagerness, Timothy's closed hand. "Now I've taken a liking to the pair of you. Just be handing over sixpence, boy, and the wee jug's yours." He held it up. It was perhaps an inch and a half high, with a curl of faint green on the double-curve of the handle, just where the user's thumb would fall. He cradled it tenderly on his dirty palm. "It's an article any lady in the land might be proud of."

Jane nudged Timothy. He handed over the money without a thought of the careful bargaining which his father employed. They went off, beaming; they had had so little money in their lives that spending even such a modest sum was a heady business.

By now Mrs Molony had sold her pig. She beckoned to them from the end of the street. It was simple for Jane to slip the jug into the bosom of her gown, padding it within a fold of her shift, but more difficult to explain away the carefully carried parcel of cabbage leaves. However, Timothy collected some more leaves dropped near one of the stalls, and pretended to be giving them to the donkey. Mrs Molony mounted the cart and drove away, the children and Brandy following behind while she smiled at everyone who caught her eye, and even at those who did not.

One of the people who did not acknowledge her was a tall decently-clad farmer. He looked at Timothy and shook his head. When Timothy seemed puzzled, he jerked his thumb in Mrs Molony's direction, tapped his forehead, and made a little screwing motion with his fingers. If he had spoken, he could not have uttered a clearer warning. "Crazed. Mad. Watch yourselves."

Timothy almost dropped his honey package. Yet he was not really surprised, and the fear which had been waiting to come into the light was only confirmed when a woman stopped near him, under pretence of picking up a tattered rag of newspaper, and muttered: "Don't believe a word she's telling you. She's away in the head this long time past, and she's never had but the one son and he—"

The donkey brayed and the vital words were lost.

Smiling and bowing Mrs Molony swept down the road. When they reached the cottage, she went in, leaving the children to attend to the donkey. Timothy told Jane what he had heard.

Jane went on stroking the donkey's velvety grey nose. "She's been so kind and so happy—" She broke off, trying to find words. "But then other times she'd talk like a different person, and her eyes would stare. One night she sat looking into the fire and talking as if she saw—saw visions in it. About John Capple. Then every time she talked of her children she'd put different names on them—" Her fingers stopped their stroking. "But one name was always the same: Johnny."

Timothy shivered. "Johnny — John — John Capple."

Jane laid her cheek against the donkey and cried, "Oh I wish we were away and at Foyleside."

"We'll go this very evening. You be getting the water from the well—anything at all to look busy, and I'll put my wits to work."

The only possessions they had in the cottage were shawl and plaid and pack. Timothy brought in turfs, and after putting his bed to rights made great play of searching for a flea. "I'd as lief change the bedding."

Mrs Molony did not look up from the pot she was stirring. "Away and get hay from the shed."

Timothy gathered up bag and plaid and shawl along with the old hay and went out.

As arranged, Jane came in: "Maybe I'd best tether the ass at the far corner. The geese have fouled the pasture hereabouts."

"Put the creature anywhere it pleases you, daughter."

Jane's heart thudded painfully. She gave the woman a quick hug. "We bought something for you at the fair. It's on the dresser. You be looking at it while we're out." She ran through the doorway feeling inexpressibly mean, while behind her rose Mrs Molony's murmur of pleasure.

By the time she reached the far corner of the field Timothy and Brandy were already there with the donkey. They hobbled him with extra knots, so that if Mrs Molony wanted to follow them with the cart time would be wasted.

This done, they ducked through the hedge and went at a rush down the road. Once round the corner they could not see whether or not she had even come to the cottage door, and soon neared the spot where they must pass the cave mouth. "I thought it was miles off," panted Timothy. "Oh Jane, put spurs to your heels. We've got to be right away from it before nightfall."

They had hardly passed it when there was a trit-trot trit-trot of hooves behind them. They had no time to do more than shrink back into the hedge before the vehicle turned the corner—a well-turned out gig.

"Thanks be," breathed Jane.

It stopped beside them and the farmer who had gestured to Timothy as they left the fair looked down at them. "So you've done a roundabout. And not before time. The poor soul's crazed. Climb in, and the dog with you. I'd not leave any child in a house belonging to John Capple's mother." He clicked his tongue at the sturdy cob between the shafts and they jogged on. "Now and again he comes back to her—at least she never lacks. There's a tale he's stuff hidden in the cave, but so far there's none been bold enough to go seeking it, or cunning enough to catch him."

The children did not look at each other. Jane said in a quavering voice, "She—she was very kind—"

"So she might be, but who's to tell when her fine Johnny will be back?" He looked them over. "Now—what under the shining sun are you on the road alone for?"

The Foyleside tale was retold. The farmer gave a wry laugh. "We'll just be hoping you've your bet on the right horse. You're halfway there anyway,

and tonight you'll be in safer shelter than Mrs
Molony could afford you."

So that night, six miles from the cave, they slept
secure, and next morning started out with well-
lined stomachs, enough potato farls and cold bacon
to carry them through the day, and clear directions
on the road they must take through the town of
Enniskillen and beyond it towards Foyleside.
The farmer ended: "The quickest way would be
through the Gap, but it's a narrow lonely kind of
place that John Capple favours. The low road by
Ballyquin is longer, and a deal safer."

As they went through Enniskillen, where shops
held much better goods than any they had seen in
Beleady, Jane said: "I'm glad we left presents with
Mrs Molony. She was laughing and cooing over
them when I ran out."

"I left a message on a scrap of the *News Letter*
that I picked up at the fair when I was getting
cabbage leaves."

"How did you write it?"

"With a sharp bit of charred wood. It was smudgy
as if I'd done it with Brandy's tail. Maybe someone
would read it to her. The spelling was very hard."
He cleared his throat and recited: "With affectionate wishes and gratitude from Jane and Timothy.
We will remember you always."

"That was beautiful—like in a romance." Jane
choked. "I wish she could have had a good son
like the ones she told me about instead of John
Capple. Oh Timothy, why do things have to be so
sad?"

Timothy felt the guinea in his pocket, and shook

his head. That was a question he could not answer. In silence they went over the bridge and into the green and well-wooded country beyond it. They would be heading north now, and must remember to avoid the Gap, even if it were the direct route— to Foyleside.

Chapter Seven

THE HIGHWAYMAN

IT WAS THE pleasantest day they had yet enjoyed.
They appeared to be well away from any danger
of recognition, they had been fed for over a week,
it was easy to take direction from the lake, the sun
shone and the hills were low. Deep in talk of what
would happen, or had happened, at Foyleside,
they wandered slowly towards the north, aided
more by milestones and signposts than by Timothy's

map which showed practically no names for this stretch of their journey.

Evening was almost upon them and they were looking for a place in which to sleep when they caught up with a drover and his unruly herd. Timothy hung back for a moment, making certain that the man was a stranger to him, and then the bullocks panicked and turned downhill. The children and Brandy acted instinctively, spreading across the road to stop the beasts before the whole mass stampeded. By that time the drover had edged the slower bullocks into a side road and under his instructions they soon had the whole herd once more looking in the same direction. The children would have passed on but the man, a burly fellow with a face red as the rising sun, called: "Hi there, gi' us a hand. My dog's behind in Enniskillen, and I'm lost for want of help."

Timothy said: "We're making for my uncle's farm on Foyleside."

"Och ay, I guessed you weren't from here-abouts—I know every man, woman and child in these townlands, but this'll only take you maybe three miles out of your way, and there'll be a bed and a meal at the end of it or my name's not Joseph McAttassey."

The name clinched it: neither of them had ever heard of anyone called McAttassey. They came to heel behind the cattle like well-trained dogs, and the bullocks realized it was useless to play any more tricks. Unfortunately the three miles turned out to be more like six. Still, the thought of free board and lodging—and Mr McAttassey's conversation—

kept their spirits up. He whiled away the miles
with talk of droving cattle over the north-west.
He said he knew every drover in this corner of
Ireland. They did their best to look blank when
he talked of Sligo and Beleady, and he was so
happy to have two listeners that he never noticed
how the mention of Will Maguire wiped all the
polite interest from their faces. "He did me an ill
turn once over a roan heifer and laughed in my
face. He'd his friends about him, so there was
little I could do. I never set eyes on him again till
a fortnight or so back." He was so deep in his story
he missed how Jane's cheeks lost their rosiness.
"This time he was tearing mad over a lad of his
who'd run away—small blame to him." He grinned
at the children. "I couldn't but be pleased to see
him get the worst of it, 'for', says he, 'Devil take
me if the lad doesn't show a clean pair of heels
before I'd the words out to send him packing.
Well for him he's out of reach of my blackthorn
stick, and there let him stay for all I care.' And
with those words he turned on his heel and left
me." He nudged Timothy in the ribs. "What'd
you make of that? In a pelter because what he
wanted hadn't happened just to his say-so! The
lad is well rid of him."

They were too full of a kind of regretful relief
to answer. He talked them up to his own tiny farm,
set in rough hill pasture, and between them they
got the tired cattle into a field.

He seemed to live alone, but the fire was bright,
and beside it a pot simmered. McAttassey rubbed
his hands. "Susan's left bacon and cabbage stew,

God bless her for the best sister ever a man had."

They supped well, and afterwards were given a choice between loft or shed for sleeping quarters. When Jane was overcome by sleepiness, Timothy swallowed down his own yawns and tried to seem interested in the drover's endless catalogue of bargains. He also heard that it was little wonder Will Maguire was ill-mannered, for he was henpecked by his new wife and would have less time in future to go running the roads looking for boon companions—or lost boys, come to that. "The packman Barney Doggart was telling me about the wife."

Timothy remembered Bridie's mention of the packman. "Wasn't Barney Doggart on the road by Beleady not long since?"

"Sure, you're miles off it, boy. He was clean through Enniskillen this very day and making north like yourselves. I have a notion he was going by Ballyquin." He gave Timothy a long direct look. "You'll know him then?"

"There's not many in the north-west doesn't know Barney."

"Ay. So. Well, them that asks no questions gets told no lies." It was the nearest he got to a direct inquiry about their names or their business.

After a pause he was off on another track. He talked until far into the night, and the stars had begun to fade in a greenish dawn sky before Timothy lay down in the hay. He was too drowsy by now to feel anything acutely, but his mind was divided between relief that his father had given up thought of pursuit, and a dull ache of regret that his own parent cared so little for him. Still, he had known that for a long time now— On this hard pillow he fell asleep.

When he woke, McAttassey was making breakfast. This consisted of bacon and cabbage drained from last night's stew and fried in bacon fat. McAttassey grinned as he watched their faces. "Lorry gorry me, it's a pleasure for a lone man to feed you."

Jane rinsed the bowls and brought in water. Timothy heaped turfs at the side of the hearth. McAttassey gave them what remained of the evening's farls. He also pointed out the two ways open to them "—if you're still for the north.

"Go back the way we were along last night, and you'll be on the Ballyquin road again. Or just be climbing over the lift of the hill and there's the Gap below you. John Capple's been known to lurk thereabouts, but he held up some poor body on the low bridge beyond Enniskillen yesterday morning, so he could be away back to thon cave of his."

The thought that John Capple was probably going in the opposite direction made up Timothy's mind before Jane could speak. "We're for the Gap then. My uncle will be needing us."

"Safe journey now, and a welcome at the end of it." As they crossed the weedy field he shouted: "And if ever you need a body to speak well of your droving, be sending him to McAttassey of Tamnaghloney."

"But Timothy, you know we'd our minds made up—not the Gap. He—John Capple—"

"He's gone the other way—you heard that for

yourself. And anyway the Gap's sure to be all right in full day, and it's so much the quicker way."

She nodded resignedly, and looked over her shoulder at the farm. "The stew was different from Granny's, maybe I'll be able to make it for your uncle. Granny says if you want to please a man make sure his belly's well-lined first."

"Brandy's well fed too, lively as a pup."

They stepped briskly up the hillside, each concealing a small misgiving. Jane was worrying about the Gap. She liked the sound of it as little as she liked the country round Bridie's cottage or John Capple's Cave. Timothy was still a little sore over the new proof that his father cared as little for him as—yes, as he for his father. Suppose at Foyleside— Only he dared not think of that, simply must press forward and get there, hoping, as McAttassey had said, that a welcome would meet them at the end of their journey.

Soon they had climbed beyond the fields and came on to open moorland where grass and heather fought for supremacy. Higher than the grass were the black peat-hags between which cotton grass waved its woolly plumes and sphagnum moss sank below even the lightest tread. It was deliciously soft after their long road walking, but when they hurried the black bog water splashed up and further streaked their weather-beaten clothes. "If only I'd a nice clean river and the day was bright I'd wash out my gown and hang it on a hedge to dry."

"Uncle won't mind a wee thing like stains from bog water."

"Granny's always saying that you must make a good first impression. She said that in Lord Drumlin's they'd never look twice at a girl seeking dairy work if she had a dirty tucker or nails so black you could nearly grow parsley in them."

"Uncle—" "Granny—" "Uncle—" They bickered amicably as they threaded their way through the maze of shoulder-high peat-hags, eyes downcast to watch the treacherous footing.

"We should be near the top and able to see the way. McAttassey said—" Timothy stopped. "If it's not the mist! I was thinking the sunrise was a watery one." He began to unstrap his plaid as a thin ripple of mist flowed downhill, eddied about them, and, like the incoming tide, retreated a short space, as if gathering strength to send down a stronger wave. Brandy came bounding back to them, every hair hung with moisture.

"We'd best go back," said Jane.

"No, no. We've only to go up the next wee bit and then we'll be over. He was saying two miles, and we've done the half of that."

"His three miles last night was nearer six. And we never wanted to go by the Gap at all. Let's go back now, quick, before we're lost."

Timothy would hear none of it. They stood there, arguing, while the mist thickened about them. Soon they were shivering with cold. "You'll get a fever again. Or we'll meet John Capple. I've no notion to the Gap. It—it's—"

"A bad place," finished Timothy for her. "You're forever saying that."

"But I've been right. They all *were* bad places."

She shook his arm. "We'll only be wasting half a day if we go to Ballyquin. There's no great hurry. Why"—her fear made her speak the words she had kept bottled up until now—"why, your uncle mightn't want us when we get to Foyleside, at all. So let's go safe and easy."

"Of course he'll want us. He must." Timothy caught her arm in his turn and forced her uphill relentlessly. "You don't know what you're talking about."

"No more do you. You've never set eyes on him. He's never written you a letter or sent a token. He could be dead and buried and forgotten for all you know. Timothy—Timothy—" She was crying now, panicked by her own words which sank into the clinging moisture and were lost, though the sense of them went on echoing through each of their minds. Panting, struggling they fought their way up the slope and suddenly, just as Timothy felt his legs would give way under him, the wind baffed in their faces and they were on a bare level stretch with peat-hags falling away on either side of them. Presumably they had reached the summit. "Now who was a crybaby?" said Timothy unkindly. "We've only to go down there—" He waved at the whiteness below them and as if at the prophet's word the mist parted, and they saw below them a dark ravine, filled with green-black pines. The sough of wind in the branches came up to them, and through it the voice of pulsing water as it hastened through the Gap towards the sunny lakeside country they had left yesterday.

Then, quickly as a transformation scene, every-thing was blotted out under a fresh mist-billow and the rough chorus of wind and water and tossed foliage became a distant mutter.

"You said we'd be going through the Gap in sunlight. Not in the wet and rain. Anything could be there. Anything at all." She tore her arm from his grasp and fled downhill at a tangent trying to get away from the sinister trees into the more open country which must lie beyond the Gap. Terrified of losing her Timothy followed, but she had the start of him, and in that clinging whiteness he could see no target at which to aim. Brandy, thinking it all a game, circled him, uttering yaps of excitement, almost tripping him half a dozen times.

His silly anger was swamped with fear of losing Jane. Why, she might tumble and break her neck, or be drowned in a boghole, or fall straight into a footpad's hands. Anything in the world might happen to her and it would be his fault. He plunged downhill, stopped to listen. Heard nothing, went on again. How light-footed she was. Or was she already in that boghole? "Brandy, seek her, boy, seek!" But Brandy was on the scent of a hare and could not wait. Faint on the echo of Timothy's cry came an exclamation, almost a gasp—then silence.

"Jane—" He blundered on round a couple more peat-hags, over a quaking blanket of moss, and came once more on to the heathery, grassy type of upland they had left on the other side of the hill. Here the mist had thinned to drizzle, and here, only a few yards before him, Jane sprawled, arms upflung, one ankle caught in a heather clump. As he bent over her she began to gather herself up. "No—breath—left in—me—" Timothy tried to raise her but no sooner was she upright against him than she crumpled. "My knee! It's broken."

While Brandy fussed anxiously up behind him he let her down among the springy heather and pushed back her ragged skirt to reveal legs as dirty as the fabric. The left knee lay at a slight angle with a lump on its inner side. She thrust him away as he would have touched her. "No, no." She tried to flex it and beads of sweat sprang out on her freckled nose. "It won't bend. Oh Timothy—if I can't walk to Foyleside—"

He knelt, holding her quiet, trying to recall a memory in exact detail. Once Papa had dislocated a finger, and, his face a sickly pallor, had extended his hand to Timothy. "The relief'll be almost worth the hurt. Jerk it while I hold the wrist. Pull like the devil." Terrified, Timothy jerked. His father grunted as if the breath had been driven out of him, and—the joint clicked into place.

His father had given one of his rare grins. "The Almighty's a powerful good joiner, but I'd lief not have to prove it every day of the week."

Timothy, muttering soothing words he could never recall, worked it out afresh. This was like Papa's finger, and it was a dislocation, not a break. The gristle had sprung out of place in Jane's knee so now he must make the opening wider to let it spring back. Despite her wail he crooked the knee sideways and away from the injury and gave a sharp tug. There was an audible click. Jane lay among the wet heather. "It's like heaven. What'd you do?" Gingerly she bent it. Delight flooded her face. "It works— if only I can stand—" She put her foot carefully to the ground. "It—it's a wee thing sore, but if I go very carefully for a minute—" She began to hobble down the hillside, turning once to say, "I'm sorry. I shouldn't have said what I did."

"Nor me neither."

They had been so preoccupied that they only saw now that they had come well below the mist and were on the verge of the dark pines which lined the Gap.

Jane cocked her head sideways. "Listen, there's a horse. Suppose it's your Papa. I said we should never have come here. It's a bad place, bad as the cave."

"He was telling McAttassey he'd never hunt us again." But all the same, he drew her down deep among the heather tussocks beside a rill of water. "Not a cheep out of you or Brandy, mind that." He pointed to a whin bush further along the slope and slightly below them. "I'll be watching from there, where I'll see the turn of the road."

He reached the bush and waited, his heart thudding against his side, but the horse that came into view was black, and the rider thicker-set than Will Maguire. Yet something was familiar: the turn of his head and the curve of the long

mouth smiling emptily at a joke known only
to himself. Give Mrs Molony ragged elf-locks
of black hair and clap a cocked hat on them and
you would have his effigy. This was John Capple.

Timothy prayed that the two above him would
not stir. His own frightened breathing came so
fast that he was sure it must sound louder than
the wind in the trees. The horseman passed a
few yards below him without looking left or right,
though for a horrid moment as the horse tossed
his head and blew sharply through his nostrils,
Timothy heard a rustle, as if Jane were having
difficulty in holding the dog down. However,
the rider went steadily on to the top of the Gap
just below Timothy, where the bank was cut
back into the hill to allow slightly more room
on a dangerous corner, and here he halted. Timothy
heard the horse snuffle and snort and its rider
snarl a low warning. Then both were silent,
while the hanging woods and the stream in the
little gorge between them kept up a chorus of
wind and water. It had been easy to hear the
metallic ring of a horseshoe through those voices,
but footsteps would be inaudible. If anyone came
up the road on foot, the lurking horseman must
surprise him. And Timothy was the only one who
could utter a warning. The minutes crept past
and no one came. Timothy prayed that the horseman would become impatient and move on,
leaving the road clear for them. Time had never
weighed so heavy, and what Jane must be suffer-
ing—yet he dared not move. Almost at the same
instant as he heard a stirrup clink when the horse

shifted, shuffling steps came up the road, and into plain view came Barney Doggart, the packman.

Brandy must have seen him too. He bounded out of hiding and came down the hillside at speed to greet an old friend. In terror for the dog's safety Timothy yelled: "Brandy!"

The packman looked suspiciously about him and halted, stick uplifted. "Who's there?"

Timothy shouted: "Watch out! Capple! Capple!"

The packman hesitated, then made for the bank above the stream, where rocks and trees and brushwood would hopelessly impede even the best of horsemen. As he reached the loose stone wall the black horse was almost upon him, and John Capple's pistol was already cocked when Brandy bounded on to the road. In terror for his friends, hardly knowing what he did, Timothy flung his precious pack full at the rider. It missed the man and struck the horse's flank, making the beast start in panic. A shot rang out, whining like a savage insect in that hollow place. The packman went over the wall like a rabbit. Brandy yelped when a flailing hoof touched him and leapt to attack—from behind. John Capple wrestled with the frightened horse, too busy to fire again, cursing, swearing vengeance, sawing savagely on the bit until his mount reared and screamed.

Jane, faced with the reality of her long-dreaded nightmare, screamed too, and in instinctive defence snatched at the stones in the runlet beside her and threw them in wild handfuls. Some rattled harmlessly through the trees, some spattered on the road. None did the slightest damage except to the horse's nerve. Despite all his rider could do, he bolted southwards, stumbling and stamping over Timothy's pack. As he fled, Jane, beside herself with terror, got to her feet, though whether to throw the better or to run she did not know, and out of the corner of her eye saw on the north side of the Gap a heavy coach toiling upwards.

The whole scene swam before her. She lifted to her mouth hands which did not seem to belong to her and called in a voice she did not recognize, "John Capple! John Capple!" She gestured towards the south of the Gap.

Timothy had heard her. As the clatter of the horse's hooves faded on the steep hill, he ran forward to meet the coach. The cracked blast of its horn rang out before it rounded the corner, and Timothy leapt clear to balance on the loose stone wall. The coachman leant sideways to address him: "What's all the shouting for? Is it Boney himself who's after you? Or is it just a beggar's trick to cadge a ride?"

"Down the road. His horse bolted with him!"

"Who, you bogtrotter you? *Who?*"

"John Capple on his black horse. Armed."

There was a babble of female voices from within the coach, and over them a man's authoritative tones. "No reason to trouble yourselves, ladies. Keep down and away from the windows." The speaker opened the door and sprang out— a brisk young lieutenant in the uniform of the Inniskilling Dragoons.

"Coachman, take me up with you. I'm a better

shot than any man on a bolting horse." As the coachman hemmed and hawed, he jumped up beside him. "Go now, or I'll take the reins from you. My sergeant on the outside seat is armed too and the best shot in the regiment."

The coachman wanted nothing to do with highwaymen. He disliked even more fervently the firearms so freely brandished near him. "I'll stick to the driving—"

"Hurry, or there'll be no reward for any of us."

The word "reward" acted like a key in a stiff door. The coach went down the road at four times the speed it had come up, the lieutenant calling as he passed Timothy: "None the worse, are you? Good lad. But get that dog out of the road before he brings someone down." He tossed a scatter of silver coins on the ground.

As the coach swept round the further corner the sergeant shouted: "I wouldn't have missed this for a shot at Boney himself. Trust the Dragoons— we'll have—" The words were lost. The voices of pines and water once more took possession of the Gap.

Timothy looked down on his crushed pack and then turned to meet Jane as she hobbled towards the road. She flung her arms about him. "Timothy." She clung as if she would never leave go, her hands icy through his thin shirt.

"And is neither of you giving a thought to me?" Barney's wizened face appeared above the wall.

"But we did! We shouted."

"God love you, boy. Can you not take a joke? But for you I'd have been meat for the hoodie

crows. I'll remember it to you to my dying day."
He looked narrowly at them, taking in Jane's
awkward gait as she limped forward to the battered
pack in the road. "Best for us to get clean away.
Others can deal with John Capple and spend
the reward—and little good such money'll do them.
But first, what's amiss with the leg, daughter?
Down on the grass here, and let's have a look."

His hands were small, neat-boned as a woman's,
and they hurt much less than Timothy's had done.
"H'm, no bones broken, but you'll hirple for a
day or two. What you need is a stout bandage—the
hem of a petticoat or suchlike—though by the
looks of you—"

Jane flushed scarlet. "I've not got one, but
if you just shut your eyes a wee minute—"

In a very short time she called: "There, will
that do?" She wriggled herself straight inside
her gown and gave him a dingy shift.

"We-ell. It's stout linen anyways." He tore it
into strips and bound up the knee expertly. "That
and my stick will hold you bravely."

Timothy, with Brandy in eager attendance,
was picking up the dragoon's shillings and his
own scattered goods. The pack itself was crushed,
the map torn, the box shattered in pieces, the
clothes alone little worse. He gathered the pieces
of wood together, then untied the roll of brocade.
Miraculously the little bone and ivory trifles
were still intact but the pearl moon on the lid of
the box had fallen from its setting. He searched
along the road margin and had almost given up
hope when an iridescent "O" of pearl glinted

at him, more precious at that moment than any
of the shillings.

The packman came over. "Ay, you've a right
muddle there." He sorted the stuff and tucked
it all up in Timothy's spare shirt. "That'll do
till I think of something better. Let's get out
of this. I'd never any notion to the Gap with or
without John Capple in it."

They went downhill at Jane's pace towards
a long green glen scattered with white cottages.
They had left the mist behind them and were
now in pale sunshine. At the foot of the hill Jane
looked back, and, as if talking to herself, murmured,
"Mrs Molony."

Barney lifted his eyebrows. "Why under the
shining sun—"

Jane did not reply. She wondered what would
happen to Mrs Molony now. If she would go
on smiling. And what the neighbours would do
and say. She shivered.

The packman asked no more questions, merely
led them off the main road and for about half a
mile along a close-hedged lane, then stopped by
a hazel coppice, which was threaded by a stream.
"No one would ever look here for you." He waved
down their protests. "What you need's a sleep.
Here—" He rummaged in his capacious side
pocket and brought out potato bread and two
apples. "Get that into you first. I've one or two
houses to call at but I'll be back long before the
light fails with news of a night's lodging."

"You wouldn't be telling—"

He straightened to his full five feet nothing,

his little dark eyes flashing. "Dear help me, didn't you save my skin?" He dabbed a finger at Jane. "You're Jane Kearney, runaway, and you"— his finger moved to Timothy—"are Will Maguire's Timothy, another runaway. I've no cause to love Grandmother Kearney nor Will Maguire neither. Where you're going is your business—and only my guess. No one on this earth will get your business nor your whereabouts nor my guess out of me. Now do you believe me or will I go on my knee-bones to the cabbage-witted, ram-stam pair of you?" He grinned at their embarrassment, revealing brown stumps of teeth. "Dear help us, you're that young, the mother's milk not dry on you yet."

Subdued, they went into the heart of the little wood, and first tethering Brandy, lay down on Timothy's plaid. Until their heads touched the mossy grass they had not realized how tired they were. At some unknown time afterwards Timothy found he was lying on his back looking into a mesh of gold-dappled leaves—it must be evening. He sat up. Brandy opened one eye and stretched. Jane still slept, unkempt curls loose on the grass. Before she stirred, Barney Doggart came into the little thicket.

His wiry legs moved with a new spring, his face was crumpled in a gleeful smile. "They got him. I heard it all from the coach coming the other way—just a mile from the Gap the two dragoons shot him down like the rat he was. But I—I was uttering not one word of the two childer who'd been in the Gap."

He bustled them up, disregarding Jane's shudder, Timothy's gasp, for it is one thing to fear an evil man and quite another to know you have helped to bring him to his death. "I've got a place for the night for the lot of us—so long as Brandy minds his manners. Tomorrow you can go to Fair Head in Antrim or Mizzen Head in Cork, and I'll ask no questions, but tonight I'll see you safe bestowed. Best to lie quiet till the shouting's over."

They followed meekly out of shade into mellow evening light, happy to leave someone else to make plans and take decisions, though it still was hard to forget the day's happenings. Something of this must have showed in their faces, for Barney halted and said almost gently: "Death's cruel. But it comes to all of us and there's no call to make every day a misery by thinking of it. John Capple only fell into the pit he dug for himself." He pinched Jane's cheek. "Just be thinking of supper."

Chapter Eight

THE TINKERS

AT AN EASY pace, for Jane's knee, though better,
was still stiff, he took them by a maze of side
roads and overgrown loanings across the breadth
of the valley floor. If they had sought to borrow a
magician's cloak of invisibility, they could have
done no better. Barney seemed very pleased
with himself. "The pair of you need to be hidden
till the fussation over John Capple dies down.

Gossip runs quicker than his black horse ever did."

They came at last to a shallow glen in the further hillside. Its entrance was screened by silver birches growing amidst feathery bracken fronds, through which a track led to a clearing where two tinkers had camped. Their donkey was tethered, and their fire crackled cheerfully under a black pot. A tawny-haired young man looked up from securing a tarpaulin and raised a hand in greeting. His wife, perhaps some four years older than Jane, stopped stirring the pot and nodded shyly, black lashes lowered.

The two children gave an equally silent greeting. Barney, however, clearly saw himself as master of ceremonies, and bustled round. To the man, whom he called Rusty, he gave a bottle; to the girl he tossed a pullet. "Chop it up fine first, Shula, so's it mixes in well." He hauled in his other pocket and brought out two onions and a bunch of parsley and thyme. "Throw them in too, the very smell's enough to make your mouth water." He slipped off his pack. "Well, Shula, which will it be—a red ribbon or a green one?"

"Wait till we've supped. Then red it'll be."

Jane, who had often watched tinkers near her home from a secret vantage point, and knew how they resented strangers, looked on with amazement.

He caught her eye. "Me and Shula's old acquaintances. You might even say I was the first to see that black head of hers. Her mother came selling clothes pegs at the farm where I'd my pack open, and her pains started early, so she birthed

Shula in the hay, with me and the woman of the house as midwives. She's the nearest I've got to a daughter."

Shula spoke to Jane for the first time. Her voice was very deep for a girl's, and Jane thought how well it would croon a fretful baby to sleep. "He's got good hands."

"Then give me some of your lotion and let me prove my skill to Jane."

Shula passed the spoon to Jane and went into the tent, presently returning with a small earthenware crock.

"Now we'll see to your knee while supper's making." He came over to Jane, pot in hand. "Off with the bandage now." Then, when she had obeyed him: "It's not near as swollen as I feared, but you'll get Shula's lotion none the less." He moistened a pad of bandage in the yellow liquid and laid it on the joint. It felt deliciously cool, and breathed out a sharp aroma, much pleasanter than Granny's goose-grease. Its freshness made her feel very travel-stained. "What is it?"

"The liquor from groundsel and elderflowers boiled together. Damp that pad of linen every time it dries off."

Jane did as she was bidden, and as he had promised, the dull ache faded. She said to Shula: "It's much better than Granny's medicine." Only the hint of a dimple in Shula's smooth brown cheek betrayed her pleasure.

By now Timothy had tied Brandy at a reasonable distance from the donkey. He helped Rusty to weigh down the edges of the tarpaulin. "Not that there's a hint of wind, mind," said Rusty, "but if you've once had a tent flying away from over you at midnight you'll never let it happen again."

The first stars were already out before the stew was ready. The onions had melted to blobs of jelly, the pullet was tender as sopped bread, and parsley and thyme together added a pungent flavour to the sauce.

They ate until they were filled, dipping in for a fresh noggin of the savoury stuff until the pot was clean. Jane and Timothy had to take turns with Timothy's noggin, and also provided Brandy with scraps. Afterwards Rusty cast a great armful of new kindling on the fire and they sat watching the flames take hold. The firelight set a reddish polish on Rusty's tousled mop, made Barney's face look more than ever like worn leather, and gave a silvery lustre to Shula's black tresses. Timothy glanced at Jane: she was sunburned and hardy as he, yet among these three, he knew they did not look like true travelling people. They were merely house-bred children who chanced to be on the road.

His gaze encountered Shula's, and as if she read his thoughts she said dreamily: "You'll be finding it, though it'll not be as you think."

"How—how do you know?"

"If I knew that I'd know it all—or maybe nothing at all."

"Half the time she's making it up," said Rusty. "She's like a tailor with cloth, fitting it to all shapes. The woman of the house will give her another penny if she's promising the next child will be a fine boy. Or if it's a poor skinny old maid then there's a dark young man just round the corner. It's easy work filling an empty cup."

Shula's eyes glinted sideways at him, like a cat's. "But Barney's here the night. That makes it different. He's our friend." She leant across and touched the packman's hand. "Grandfather." The word was like a caress.

He answered it. "Indeed, daughter, you've never told me anything but the truth since you were a poor wee wean tumbled out on the rough hay." He added: "Show her the box, Timothy."

Wondering, Timothy laid bare the broken pieces of wood. Shula turned them over, and without asking permission, unrolled the green brocade. She stroked it gently, her rough fingers catching on the fabric, and looked over the little heap of woman's tools. Lastly she picked up the thread-holder and poised it in the palm of her hand almost level with her eyes, where the firelight painted its gleaming surface with amber, and darkened the rudely-scratched initials. Without taking her gaze from it, she said in a sing-song: "This is bone and it came from far away over the sea. It was old before we were born and when we're all gone to bones, like the woman who owned it, it'll be over another sea still holding thread." She stopped as if listening. "The woman went from home and this is going back the way she came." The next words came slowly, as if she had to search for them. "It'll be shown to someone with a name like hers, only not quite the same, and it'll go further than she went."

A piney stick in the fire sent a shower of sparks amongst the listeners. Shula dropped the piece of ivory as if it burned her fingers. She looked at Rusty. "This time it was true."

She was shivering like one stricken with ague. Jane made to offer her shawl, but Rusty pushed her aside and cuffed his wife soundly on one cheek. She looked at him in bewilderment, tears of shock in her eyes, then rose in a quick supple movement, scattering the worn trifles about her. "Put them away. I wouldn't wish to set eyes on them again." She almost ran to the heap of wood and began to select pieces from it to build up the fire.

"She takes the seeing too hard," said Rusty, stretching himself into a more comfortable position on the grass. "Once she's birthed a child or so she'll have other things to think about."

Jane went over to the tinker girl and put her shawl about her; they smiled at each other.

The sight of Timothy yet again collecting his small possessions made Barney exclaim: "If I'd not forgotten to cry my own wares! Bring the box here boy, and we'll see what Doggart's Patent Glue can do."

It was not hard to sort out the pieces, for the box had merely been broken into its original components. It took longer to bring the glue to the right consistency. Timothy would have lost hope long before the task was finished, but Barney kept steadily on, and as fast as one side fell off, he patiently pressed it into place again, until there stood the box and its lid, complete to the pearly moon. "Come morning and it'll be fit to pack up."

While this was going on the two girls were in the tent sorting out clothes which Shula had begged during the past week. Jane was so sleepy that her eyes soon closed. Shula drew an old frieze coat over her, and went out to join the men. By now, Timothy, never the best of musicians, was doing his best to whistle the jig tune which Barney had begun.

They romped about the fire, disturbing Brandy, ignored by the donkey and, finally, deserted by Timothy who, as a black bottle of liquor made its appearance, was pushed into the tent. He did not even remember being told to sleep. The fire sparkled, the dancers sang, Shula and Rusty and Barney drank, and the sun rose before he woke and found morning already well advanced.

Jane had been less tardy. She woke soon after dawn, filched a tattered cotton petticoat from the heap of clothes around her, tiptoed between the scattered sleepers and, having untied Brandy, limped downstream with him as escort until she found a secluded pool. A heron rose at her approach and angled its way noiselessly through the trees. Jane tried the water cautiously with her toe: it might have melted snow, so icy was it. She washed, gasping and shivering, while the level beams of early morning sun struck through the trees. She rubbed and pummelled herself with the petticoat until her whole body glowed; then, sighing, pulled on her dirty gown. The petticoat was useless now, so she buried it under a stone and turned for the camp.

Shula slipped between the boughs quietly as an otter. "Do you like washing all over?"

Jane was taken aback. "N-no. Not always. But after—after what happened yesterday—"

"Don't fret over him. He made his own end." She dabbled one strong brown foot in the water. "It's good to be washing feet and eyes, though I've no liking for the smell of water on me. I like the smell of myself."

Jane thought of how different Lady Felicia and Mrs Molony had smelled.

The older girl gave her sidelong smile. "You're not one of the travelling people. You'll be wanting a roof over you." She considered Jane's rosy face, brown curls, and thin childish neck. "When you're full grown you'll be fit to take a man's fancy." Almost mischievously she caught Jane's hand. "Quick before the men are waking."

"What—"

Shula brought her to the tent. "Wait." She picked her way between the sleeping men and came back with a bundle of old clothes. From amongst them she drew a shift of delicate cambric. Its lace edging was torn, otherwise it was quite wearable. "It was a fine lady's. I had it from her maid for looking in the teacup and seeing a stout young shopman dying for love of her." She t't-t'ted with her tongue. "Tea every day in the kitchen." She felt the delicate stuff between her fingers. "It'll be like silk on your skin. Get it on, and then we'll be finding a gown." She rummaged amongst the heap, and finally pounced on two: a leaf-brown holland, and a fine blue wool with a frill at the neck. "Take your pick. Neither would meet round my bosom." Jane chose the blue, and slipped it over her head, trembling with excitement. It was two years since she had had a new gown.

It was perhaps four inches too long and far too loose, but Shula slit the fabric with her knife and tore the hem clean off. "That'll gird it round your middle."

Jane turned herself about, preening like a bird. It was quite the prettiest gown she had ever worn. Of course the edge was now raw, it had a stain down one side and a scatter of tiny burn-holes where sparks must have touched it, but it was worlds better than the weather-beaten gown at her feet. It smelled of wood smoke mingled with a distant memory of lavender. As she was about to ask Shula how she had come by it the elder girl shook her head. "Never mind who owned it. That's over and done with."

She threw the other clothes back into the tent, and turned to the embers of the fire. As they had scraped the pot clean last night there was little to eat except the oatcake which Barney had providently hidden in his pack. Rusty, remarking that he hated eating dry, went off with a crock in his hand and returned presently with fresh milk. No one asked questions about that. Neither did they ask about the rabbit Brandy dragged in. But all agreed he was the best of dogs, and he was given a hind leg for his portion. Shula began to prepare the rest of the meat for the pot.

Jane came in for a little teasing over her finery, and Timothy looked at her with new eyes, secretly rather relieved: after all, he still had a spare shirt and breeches.

When the meal was over Timothy carefully tied up his belongings in an old stuff skirt Shula found for him. At this point Barney took command: he also was making for the north and would set them on their way. "But now let's be paying for a night's lodging." He pulled out a generous bunch of red ribbon and handed it to Shula, who immediately tied her hair back from her forehead and secured it with a bow above her ear. Rusty was handed a long packet. He shook it, grinned and made the gesture of a man tilting a drink to his mouth. "*Slainte*, Grandfather!"

Timothy whispered to Jane, "Buy something out of his pack."

"Please Barney, we've the dragoon's money— could I just be looking over what you've got?"

"When did I ever stop a young woman who'd money to spend?" He opened the pack before her.

Shula and Rusty came near and gazed down as if at a treasure chest.

Jane examined everything: needles and pins, thread and buttons, pills and potions, soap for the complexion, snuff, perfumed lozenges, ginger root, cloves and cinnamon sticks, combs and blurry looking-glasses, knives and scissors, ribbons and laces and neckerchiefs. She pursed her lips in concentration, and at last held out her hand to Timothy, who dropped into it the dragoon's silver coins. She picked a comb, a two-inch square mirror in a brass frame, a pair of scissors and a selection of spices—two cinnamon sticks, perhaps a dozen cloves and a few knobbly ginger roots, which she placed carefully on separate docken leaves. So much for Shula. She then went on to the much harder problem of choosing Rusty's gift. In the end she settled for a red cotton neckerchief patterned with yellow posies of some strange oriental flowers, a new knife and a packet of snuff.

Barney said that the dragoon's money covered this, with even a little to spare, but Jane did not wish to keep any reminder of John Capple, so she handed it all back and turned to the two young tinkers.

Suddenly she was shy. "Barney—please—"

So Barney presented the gifts and though Rusty made great play with putting on the new neckerchief while Shula looked in the glass at the set of her ribbon, and smelled each of the spices in turn, suddenly the life went out of the party, for now the friends of a night must go different ways to different destinations.

Shula said: "May you have a safe journey, whether it's over land or sea."

Timothy thought how Jane and he were going to a kinsman's house, and how Shula and Rusty would go wandering all their days. Suddenly he said something which he had not known was lying in his mind. "There was never a welcome in my father's house like the one we had from you last night."

In silence they walked out of the glen to the road, and all that day Barney kept them company, carefully suiting his pace to Jane, for although much improved, her knee was not completely healed.

Chapter Nine

TO FOYLESIDE—AND FURTHER

UNDER HIS GUIDANCE they went through the next village, and were told to wait on the far side of a hayfield while he made a round of his customers. "Here's a bite of soda bread and a bottle of butter-milk to stay your stomachs. Tomorrow I'll set you on the road to Foyleside. I'll be visiting someone who buys things the Revenue men never set eyes on."

Obediently they settled in the sunlight in the shelter of the stone wall, Brandy stretched happily beside them. Somehow they dreamed and dozed the hours away until Barney returned in good spirits, grinning over business well done. He had found lodging for them in a stable not far away. As it rained that night they were glad of cover and by dawn a thin sunlight was filtering through the clouds, though trees hung heavily.

By now Jane's knee was almost better so she kept up easily with the others although the way led uphill. Soon the road forked, and here Barney paused. "I've business in Dungiven that won't wait, so I'll be going right, and if you want Foyleside you'll have to take the other fork. Jump up on the bank, boy, and tell us what you see."

Timothy scrambled up. Beyond well-tilled fields wound a broad river, silvery now in the wan light. He looked down at Barney. "It's Foyleside?"

"It is so. All you've got to do is find the right corner. Upper Dolaghan, wasn't it? As I remember it's about four miles north from here—but I'm too pressed for time to lead you."

He pinched Jane's cheek, told her to brisk up, flourished his stick, turned a corner and was gone.

Jane had indeed turned pale, realizing for the first time what a weight she had placed on Timothy's shoulders, forcing him to seek help from a man who did not know she existed. She shut her eyes and prayed: "Let Timothy's uncle be there, and let him welcome us both."

Few people were about this damp morning, but at last they found a farmer who admitted that Dolaghan would be three or four miles away. Encouraged, they asked at the next two farms, and at last got clear directions. "Two miles ahead and down a loaning on your left with trees meeting over it."

Relieved, they continued down the road: well, at least the place was still there, but—but they had been so certain that all they had to do was arrive at Foyleside and almost bump into the house They walked with a hollow fear growing inside them, and at last when just such a lane loomed up on their left could hardly believe it. Together they turned to the cottage on the other side of the road, where a tall comely woman stood in the doorway. At the sight of them the colour ebbed from her cheeks. "Lord love us, boy, if you're not the dead spit of Molly Erskine."

From a dry mouth Timothy said: "She was my mother. I—we—we've come seeking my uncle Alexander Erskine at Upper Dolaghan."

She made a small inarticulate sound of sympathy. "Och childer, Alexander left Upper Dolaghan a month since."

"But we've come all this way to find him—he's *got* to be there." Jane sank down on the floor, her new blue gown ruffling about her. She began to shiver. "I can't go back, Timothy. Not *ever*!"

The woman gave something between a sigh and a laugh. "You'd think we were at a wake. Alexander's alive and well, thanks be." She patted Jane's shoulder. "You stay here in the warm, and you"—she turned to Timothy—"don't go breaking your heart over nothing, but if you're to see Upper Dolaghan as it was in your Mama's day put spurs to your heels." She touched his hair gently. "I'm

Mary MacSorley, and I knew your mother long ago. I'll be tending the wee girl. There's no nightmare waiting at the lane's end. Away now and see for yourself." Timothy ran back to the lane with Brandy close behind him. A waggon loaded with timber was near the top of it, but he passed it without a look, and came at a gallop through the trees on to a tiny landing, heaped with building materials, on the very verge of the Foyle, whose wide waters were now dancing in afternoon sunlight.

He looked around, trying to piece together his mother's tales: the lively water, the green slopes, and, not a hundred yards from the jetty, a snugly thatched cottage, guarded by white gateposts and two dark-green Irish yews. The garden was a tangle of sweet rocket and buttercups, all half-strangled in the fallen sprays of a pink rose. Behind the house were lichened apple trees, already laden with tight green fruit. This was the dream come true. Only when he came close to the gate he saw that the windows were uncurtained and the front door kicked wide. Molly Erskine's home was now tenantless.

He stood at gaze, reliving the hopes and tasting the reality. Only he did not yet know exactly what the reality was. Brandy thrust a cold nose into his palm and whined, conscious that something had gone amiss.

From the lane came sounds of wheels and hoof-beats and a loud adjuration: "Take it easy, you fool beasts, you!" And round the corner jolted the load of timber he had passed unseeing on the road.

The driver jumped down. "Admiring the view, eh? Well, it's free the now, but come Christmas and young Mr Lanchester—him that's heir to Sir John—will have his fine new house where the cottage is. Just for the fishing, mind you. He took a notion to it and didn't his Papa put money enough to buy it into his hand then and there." He sniffed. "They never thought of asking Alexander Erskine whether he wanted to leave—and a brave decent soul he is. Gone over to Tullynagardy now."

"He's my uncle."

"Then you'll be—"

Timothy and Brandy were already on their way up the lane. Tullynagardy—Tullynagardy— Not until he reached the road did he remember that this was the name Jane had pointed out on the very edge of the map. Suddenly he thought of Shula's words: "You'll be finding it, though it'll not be what you think." And with that memory came another: that he would show the ivory thread-holder to someone with a name like his mother's but not exactly the same.

With that thought his mind steadied, and though he felt bruised inside him, he could bear the ache. Perhaps he would always long for the house on Foyleside, but Tullynagardy still remained, and his uncle was alive. He even forgot to be angry with young Mr Lanchester, and into his mind drifted the picture of Jane, crumpled in the folds of her blue dress. Until then he had not realized how brave and trusting she had been. To Brandy he said: "But I'll make up every single minute of it to her. You see if I don't."

Together they tumbled into the kitchen where Jane was putting bowls on the well-scrubbed table. A look of relief came over Mrs MacSorley's face. "You've seen for yourself and you've not broken your heart over it. After all, Alexander was only a tenant. Thanks be, this place is my son's— he's away buying cattle the now—so no My Lord This-and-That will be shifting him. Lucky for Alexander he'd Tullynagardy to fall back on, left by the cousin who died without a child."

"Mama never talked much about it."

"It was no more than a name to her. The will was made after she ran off to Sligo." She gave a little sideways smile. "I was twelve years older than her and she thought me a staid kind of being, and I"—suddenly she stooped and kissed Timothy— "she was like the wee daughter I never had."

A long look passed between her and Jane. Timothy sat silent, if not content, at least momentarily at rest in a peaceful home. In the same meditative silence they ate their meal, while the sun slanted through the windows and laid a haze of gold on every face.

Mrs MacSorley looked kindly at them. "Deary me, you two need a roof and a home as much as any childer I ever saw, but maybe—maybe—" She cleared her throat and gave them very precise details of the way to Tullynagardy, and the appearance of the cottage. "It'll be about twelve miles on and the road is clear and safe all the way. Tonight you can bed down in the loft above there."

Next morning, fortified with a day's provision of oaten bread, the children and Brandy set out.

As instructed they climbed the low hills to the east of the city of Derry and on this vantage point they stopped. There ran the coach road and there the side road towards Tullynagardy.

"You'd best put on your best breeches and clean shirt," said Jane. "I'll tie my hair with the ribbon I got at the fair." So Timothy stripped behind a whin bush while Jane pored over the map, with Tullynagardy on its very edge, and Shula's words sang in her ears. "You'll be finding it, though it'll not be as you think."

When Timothy stepped from behind his bush she was already smiling. "This time I'll not let you run down the lane alone. I'll go with you."

They turned up the side road. Only three cottages stood in this stretch, and, as Mrs MacSorley had said, the third looked towards the lough. It had a flowery hedge dangling with blossoms, and a chimney out of the middle of the roof.

Timothy's heart began to beat so fast that he could hardly untie the knot of his bundle and bring out the box. They looked at the house so long that a tall bearded man came out of the door. He considered them gravely, and even when Brandy bounded up still stood silent, as if his thoughts were far away, but at last he gave a smile which made his sad face look ten years younger. "Well, it seems the cat has got your tongues. What is it you're wanting, childer?"

Jane said in a whisper: "Show it to him, Timothy."

Timothy held out the battered box. "Mama gave it to me. I—I'm Molly Erskine's son, born after she went away to Sligo in 1798. You'll be my uncle that lived at Upper Dolaghan on Foyleside. I went there and it was just like Mama was telling me, and then Mrs MacSorley said you'd be here."

Jane had already unfurled the tattered map, and now she pointed: "Look: Tullynagardy. Please sir, we've come all the way from Sligo seeking you and—and the box there is all the proof Timothy has that he is what he says he is."

"Except this," said the big man. He put out his hand and tilted Timothy's head gently back, the better to see him. "Lord's sake, boy, looking at you is like seeing Molly again in a lad's body. You've been heavy on my mind since Seamus the fiddler told me that Molly was away and Will Maguire a hard man to live with. But you"—he considered Jane—"you're out of a different stable."

Jane flushed. "I am so. But my granny was kin to Timothy's father and no one was wanting me any more than his father's new wife wanted him. Please sir, I can milk and look after fowl and spin a little, so I'd be no charge on anyone, and Mrs MacSorley said—she said—"

"Out with it, daughter. I'll believe all Mary MacSorley ever said."

"She said she'd only the one son and he was wanting the farm more than he wanted her, and that she'd like fine to have a daughter."

He began to laugh. "It seems I can trust her with everything except a secret."

Timothy stared from one to another in puzzlement. His uncle laid a hand on his shoulder. "To cut a long story short, Mary MacSorley has pledged herself to marry Alexander Erskine this Monday fortnight."

Without giving Timothy time to reply he drew him across the yard. "Come inside. But keep the dog to heel. I've a lame bitch here and I'd not wish her to be hurted." He showed them into a big untidy kitchen whose small-paned window looked towards the lough, set the box on the table and began to unpack it.

Jane was looking about her. "It's still Foyleside and—"

Timothy cut across her. "There's the lustre jug and the delft teapot on the dresser with the rosebud on the lid."

"And the A.B.C. sampler."

Alexander looked up from the bobbin and the thread-holder which lay in his hand. "I cut the letters of her name on these, and brave and hard the ivory was too. But that's all of fifteen years ago, afore she dipped her finger in the '98 and went off with her man to Sligo. Since then, what with Boney and the Union with England and trade bad, it's a different world—but for the landlords, and they'll not alter in a thousand years. See what they did to us over Dolaghan, where Erskines have been tenants a hundred and fifty years."

He put the little objects down beside the much-travelled box. "That's one thing we'll not be leaving behind us."

Jane smiled because he had said "us", Timothy said blankly: "Why *behind* us?"

"Because we're for Americky. What living is there here on fifteen acres? Over yonder the land is wide—and cheap. We may have lost Upper Dolaghan, but it was a brave wee farm and I've money saved from it to buy land overseas. You'll need all your farming skills just as much in Americky as you did in Sligo—or I in Upper Dolaghan."

Jane was staring at the ivory thread-holder. "Shula said it would be shown to someone with a name like Timothy's mother, and that it would travel over another sea."

"And who's Shula to know all our secrets?"

They began to tell him. Brandy stretched at their feet, content because he was warm and they were happy.

More Beaver Books

We hope you have enjoyed this Beaver Book. Here are some of the other titles:

The Twelve Labours of Hercules The adventures of the hero Hercules, beautifully retold by Robert Newman; illustrated superbly by Charles Keeping

Travel Quiz A brain-teasing quiz book for all the family on all aspects of travel by plane, train and car

My Favourite Animal Stories Sad, funny and exciting stories about all sorts of animals, chosen and introduced by Gerald Durrell

The Glass Knife Gripping and intriguing story about a boy who has been reared to become a human sacrifice. Set in South America before the European discovery of the New World; by John Tully, with illustrations by Victor Ambrus

The Last of the Vikings Henry Treece's exciting story, in the saga tradition, about the young Harald Hardrada, King of Norway; with more superb illustrations by Charles Keeping

New Beavers are published every month and if you would like the *Beaver Bulletin* – which gives all the details – please send a stamped addressed envelope to:

Beaver Bulletin
The Hamlyn Group
Astronaut House
Feltham
Middlesex TW14 9AR

393623